Dog Days

JournalStone's DoubleDown Series, Book III

By

Joe McKinney

JournalStone
San Francisco

JournalStone books may be ordered through booksellers or by contacting:

JournalStone
www.journalstone.com
www.journal-store.com

ISBN: 978-1-940161-12-9 (sc)
ISBN: 978-1-940161-29-7 (hc – limited edition)
ISBN: 978-1-940161-13-6 (ebook)

Library of Congress Control Number: 2013951062

Printed in the United States of America
JournalStone rev. date: December 6, 2013

Cover Design: Paul Vaughn
Cover Art: Alfredo Lopez Jr.
Edited by: Elizabeth Reuter

This one is for Jeff, Mark and Ralph
Who lived it with me back in 1983

Dog Days

"It must be a wild place."

"Yes, the setting is a worthy one. If the devil did desire to have a hand in the affairs of men –"

"Then you are yourself inclining to the supernatural explanation."

"The devil's agents may be of flesh and blood, may they not?"

From an exchange between Holmes and Watson in Sir Arthur Conan Doyle's "The Hound of the Baskervilles"

Dog Days

My dad had me pinned to the floor. He put a finger to his lips and said, "Shhh, you'll wake your mother."

I had lurched out of sleep so suddenly, with the storm still roaring in my head, that it took me a moment to realize where I was.

"You're alright," he whispered. "It's over. Stop fighting."

I blinked at him. He was kneeling next to me, our dog Max sitting behind him, his yellow eyes focused on me, tail wagging a million miles an hour. The poor dog was so excited he could barely contain himself. Probably happy to be alive, I thought. I knew I was, because there'd come a point during the night when I seriously doubted I'd see the morning. But the fear I'd felt then was rapidly shrinking.

I looked around, took stock. The house behind my dad was dark. The air was hot and humid. I couldn't hear the hum of the air conditioners. I heard nothing but Max's impatient breathing and the sweep of his tail across the floor. I let myself go slack, all the tension fading.

"What's going on?" I asked in a whisper. "Is the power out?"

"Yes, the power's out. The water too. Probably will be for a few days. Come with me. I want to show you something."

I sat up and rubbed my arms. Hurricane Alexis had made landfall the night before, and when the wind and the rain got really bad—bad enough that the house started to shake and I honestly thought the roof would tear away and go sailing off like a kite cut from its string—my family had gone into our walk-in hall closet for shelter. It was where we stashed everything. My parents loved to throw dinner parties, and that closet was where we kept all the extra tables and chairs and fondue kits and everything else. But it was the only room downstairs that didn't have an exterior wall. My dad said we'd be safest there. So we took out all the tables and chairs, made a bed out of coats and old sweaters, and hunkered down for the storm. My mom put her arms around me and hugged me so tightly she left finger-shaped bruises on my skin.

But that was over now. The storm had passed, and we had made it through.

Moving slowly, so as not to disturb my mom, I got up and followed my dad through the hall and out to the living room, Max trotting along at my side.

"Are we gonna take down the boards?" I asked.

The day before, when the weatherman said that the storm was definitely going to make landfall at Galveston, my dad and I went around the house nailing sheets of plywood over the windows. Good thing too because the wind had snapped off one of the branches from the pecan tree in our front yard and sent it crashing into the big bay window in my mom's office. We went into the closet shortly after that. All the other boards had held though. White lines of light glowed from the edges of the windows on the front of the house, and I took that as a good sign. Daylight had come, and I'd had enough rain for a long while.

"Later," my dad said. "First, I want you to see this."

He led me to the front door, opened it, and then stood off to one side so I could look out.

"Whoa!" I said.

His smile was wide. "I know. Cool, right?"

I turned back to the doorway, stunned. We lived in a neighborhood called Brook Forest, one of the wealthier parts of

Clear Lake, a little bedroom community about midway between Houston and Galveston. My dad was a sergeant in the Houston police, but my mom was a pediatrician, and because of her we were able to live in one of the nicest homes in a neighborhood made up of nothing but nice homes. Now those gorgeously huge houses looked like islands in a sea of caramel-colored water. There was water everywhere. It came right up to the front door. We had a big brick mailbox down at the curb, but I couldn't even see it. The water was that deep. Across the street, near where his mailbox should have been, was Mr. Matheson's blue pickup truck. Except only the top two or three inches near the roof were visible above the waterline.

As I watched, a water moccasin glided by, a long black ribbon on the brown water.

Then I caught movement out of the corner of my eye and looked down. Our lawn sloped away from the house to meet the street, and so the water up near the porch was only a few inches deep. There, hundreds of red crawdads were waving their pinchers in the air, as though outraged and confused by the way they'd been uprooted from their home in the bayou down at the end of my street.

"Dad, look!"

His smile broadened. "I thought you'd like that."

We stepped out onto the porch together and Max followed along. When he saw the crawdads he jumped from the porch and splashed around in the shallow water, his mouth open and teeth bared as he tried to bite them. I noticed he kept his nose high and his tongue pulled into the back of his mouth, though. He'd dealt with crawdads before. He knew those pinchers could hurt.

One of the crawdads grabbed hold of Max's teeth and, startled, Max shook his head until it went flying off, landing with a small splash halfway across the yard. Max barked at it, and my dad and I laughed. I looked up at him and he smiled down at me, and for a moment, I thought we were fine. It felt good, standing there together in the middle of the flood, realizing that we'd come through okay. But then his smile faded and his expression turned sad and I knew that even this new adventure wasn't enough to allow him to forgive me.

Luckily neither one of us got a chance to discuss it, for just then Mr. Moore pulled up to our porch in a little aluminum boat. Mr. Moore lived down at the corner of our block in a house that looked like an old Louisiana plantation. On school days, I caught the bus at the corner under the shade of an enormous pecan tree he had in his front yard. He was kind of fat and really pale and going bald, and he looked ridiculous sitting in the boat in his white t-shirt and baby blue shorts and black socks.

"Morning, Wes," he said to my dad. "You and Meredith make it through okay?"

"Morning, Tom. I haven't had a chance to look at the roof yet, but I think we did all right. How about you and Eleanor? You guys good?"

Mr. Moore was wearing an Astros baseball hat. He took it off and wiped his bald head before answering. "Well, actually, I got a bit of a problem I was wondering if you could help with."

"Oh yeah? What's up?"

Mr. Moore looked back toward his house, and when he turned back to us, I could see he was scared.

I think my dad noticed it too.

"What's wrong, Tom?"

"Um, can you…can you see my house from there?"

We couldn't. There were trees in the way. My dad stepped off the porch and walked into the yard until he was up to his knees in the floodwater.

"Oh my God," he said.

I jumped off the porch and ran to his side. And looking down the street toward Mr. Moore's house I got my second shock of the day.

"Is that a shrimp boat?" I asked.

My dad nodded.

I couldn't believe what I was seeing. We were seven miles from the shrimp and oyster camps down in Kemah, but somehow the storm had carried one of those shrimp boats all the way from down in Kemah to the corner of my block, where it now rested in the branches of Mr. Moore's pecan tree. The tree looked like a giant trying to pull a toy boat out of the water.

"How is that even possible?" I asked.

"I don't know," my dad said. "Storm surge must have carried it here. Had to have been seven or eight feet of surge to cause this kind of flooding. I guess it could've carried a boat."

My dad turned to Mr. Moore and shrugged. "I don't know if I can do anything about that, Tom. I guess you'll just need to call your homeowner's insurance once the phones come back up. You're probably gonna need a crane to get that thing out of there."

"Huh?" Mr. Moore said. "Oh, yeah, I guess you're right."

"What's wrong, Tom?" my dad asked. "You look spooked."

Spooked was one way of putting it, I thought. Actually, Mr. Moore looked like he didn't quite have the words to say what he needed to say. He opened his mouth to speak, then stopped, looked at me, and then at my dad, and tried again. "Can you…would you come with me, Wes. Please."

"Well, sure," my dad said. "Just tell me what's wrong."

"It's…" He took a deep breath. "There's a bad smell, Wes. You know what I mean? It's real bad."

"Oh," my dad said. "Oh, okay. Come closer. Let me get onboard."

Mr. Moore turned the motor back on and coasted up to our porch. My dad climbed aboard and I tried to follow.

"Um," Mr. Moore said, holding up a hand to stop me. "I think, Mark, it'd be best if it was just your dad."

"But I want to see the boat," I said.

"No," my dad said, and right away I recognized the bark of command in his voice. It was what my mom called his cop voice. "You stay here. Take Max inside and help your mother. I'll be back in a bit."

"But Dad…"

"I said no. Now go on. Take Max inside."

Before I could say more they backed the boat up and powered off, leaving Max and me on the porch. He looked up at me and whined.

"Figures," I said. "Come on, Max. This summer's gonna suck."

I walked back inside and closed the door and sat on the stairs. Max put his head in my lap and I scratched him behind the ears, but not even he could pull me out of the misery I felt. Biggest adventure of my life and I was sitting on the sidelines.

But then there came a knock at the back door.

One I knew very well.

Max raised his head, perked his ears up, then let out a series of deep, booming barks as he ran for the back door.

I followed him through the kitchen and into the mudroom. Once there, I opened the door to see my best friend, Jeff Hefke. Behind him, tied off to the corner of my garage, was a bright orange canoe.

"Dude, is he gone?"

He meant my dad. "Yeah, he went down the street with Mr. Moore."

"That's crazy, right? You saw that?"

"The shrimp boat. Yeah, I saw it."

"Well, come on, let's go." He pointed over his shoulder at the canoe.

"Dude, I can't. My dad told me to stay here."

"Oh come on," he said. "There's a shrimp boat up a tree. How many times are you gonna get to see that?"

I laughed. He was right, of course. He usually was. Of course, him being right usually got me in trouble.

Jeff and I got in his canoe and paddled down my driveway to the street. Now that I was out in it, I really got a sense for the destruction the storm had left behind. The weatherman said that we were going to catch the dirty side of the storm, the side where the winds were strongest and the damage was usually the worst. I could believe it, looking at all this. My neighborhood had a bunch of huge trees, pines and pecan and oak and dozens others that I didn't know the name of, and nearly all of them looked like they'd lost limbs to the wind. Power lines were down. The Matheson's place, directly across the street from ours, had thousands of bright green pecan leaves plastered to its surface. And garbage of every sort, from Styrofoam cups to Coke cans to unnamable bits of plastic, floated in the current. I heard a nasty sounding metal-on-metal grinding and looked down to see that the bottom of our canoe had just scratched up the roof of Mrs. Matheson's Mercedes.

"Oh shit," I said.

"Man, we used to play kickball in this street. Can you believe it?"

"The water should drain away in a few days."

"Yeah, but I don't know if I can ever look at this place the same way again, you know?"

I did. I got it. Though I was only fourteen, I still realized that I had it pretty good growing up. I was, by any reasonable way you want to measure it, growing up rich. My neighborhood, hell, everything about my life, had always been comfortable and safe and secure. But now I was looking at that security sacked. My comfortable upbringing had just gotten bitch slapped by the Gulf of Mexico, and there I was, floating around in a canoe in the ruins of everything I thought I knew of the world.

Jeff used his paddle to push us off Mrs. Matheson's Mercedes and we got moving again. A few neighbors were outside on their front porches, most of them with stunned expressions on their faces.

I waved and a few of them waved back.

Jeff said, "What do you think the Swamp looks like?"

The Swamp was a vast expanse of undeveloped marshland at the edges of our subdivision. My friends and I spent our summer days there, our dogs at our side, our pellet guns gripped by the breach like we were Marines in the Asian jungles of World War II.

I thought of Jeff's question. What would it look like right now? The answer seemed obvious to me. It would be a sheet of brown water, punctuated here and there by clusters of trees.

Like the rest of my mental map of the world, it was in the process of reconstruction.

"You know what," Jeff said. "I bet the alligators are loving this."

I stopped paddling. I put the paddle across my lap and stared daggers into his back.

"Dude, really? You think that's funny?"

"Oh come on, Mark. It's not that big of a deal."

"Maybe not to you."

"Whatever. You can be a real pansy sometimes."

"Screw you, Jeff."

"You wish."

He laughed and went back to rowing. I did too.

We'd completed the 8th grade two weeks before and this summer was supposed to be our gateway to the Promised Land. In about ninety days we'd start high school. We were about to enter an undiscovered country of girls who actually had tits, and would probably be willing to show them to us. God help us, there was a chance we might actually get laid.

That was looming in our future.

As a reward Jeff suggested we get my dad's pistol and go out for a bit of target practice.

My dad is a cop, like I've said, and he has a lot of guns. His gun safe is one of those floor-to-ceiling jobs, with a safety lock. He thought he'd done a pretty good job of hiding the key, but I was a teenager, and of course I knew exactly where it was.

So, that first Monday of our vacation, my dad had one of those police-for-charity golf tournaments he was always doing. He was going to be gone from 6 a.m. to sometime in the late afternoon. And of course my mom was gone, working at her practice. I was left all on my own, with nothing but a key to my dad's private gun stash to entertain me.

I did what any teenage boy would do. I called over my best friend and unlocked the gun cabinet and gloated as he stood amazed at the weapons before him.

There were machine guns and long rifles and combat shotguns and even vintage military pistols spread out there before us; but what caught both our gazes, what held us transfixed, was the .357 Smith & Wesson revolver with the blued barrel and the walnut grips. Along its four-inch barrel an inscription read HOUSTON POLICE DEPARTMENT, and above the trigger the weapon's serial number read SW0191HPD, my father's badge number.

That was the Holy Grail of the gun chest.

It was a long moment before I finally reached out and took it.

"He won't know?" Jeff asked.

"He'll never have a clue," I said. "We'll have time to replace any ammunition we use."

Jeff nodded. I wrapped the gun up in a dishtowel and put it into my backpack. Then we went to the Swamp and wandered around looking for something to shoot at when we came across a ten-foot-long alligator sunning itself next to a pond that was scummed over with bright green algae.

Jeff and I had both spent plenty of time out there in the Swamp. We'd seen snakes and wild hogs and wild dogs and even fish slapping and flapping from one creek to the next. But alligators were a rarity. They usually kept to the ponds, sunken out of sight.

But this one was brazen. It rested right in the middle of the trail we were on, its mouth wide open, a challenge to any who might dare a fight.

"Let's stop here," Jeff said.

I looked from the alligator to my best friend. "No way. Let's go around."

"No." I could see his gaze shift from my face to my backpack. Then he slowly turned to face the alligator. "Those things give me the creeps. Can I shoot first?"

"It's my dad's gun."

He shrugged. "Okay, well, come on. Take it out."

I did. I took it out and loaded it from one of my dad's speed loaders and then aimed it at the base of a dead pine tree some twenty yards away.

"What are you aiming at?" Jeff asked.

"That tree."

"Why?"

I didn't answer. I knew what he expected me to do, and I didn't want to. The idea of doing it made me sick.

Finally, I said: "He's not bothering anybody. Can't we just leave him be?"

"Go over there and stand about five feet from him. See if he'd let *you* be."

"That's different. He's just a wild animal."

"That makes no sense, Mark. Just shoot him already. He's a lizard. It's not like he's gonna feel any pain."

"Animals feel pain," I said.

"Not reptiles. They've got those simplified reptile brains. You ever see a snake get run over by a car? What does it do?"

"Crawls off, usually."

"Exactly!" He threw up his hands like he was about to say, "Praise the Lord. Hallelujah!"

"Dude, that's stupid," I said. "That doesn't prove anything."

"It's a stupid alligator, man. The world's not gonna miss him. Just shoot him."

He wasn't going to let it go. That was one thing I hated about Jeff. Once he got a thing stuck in his head he'd hound a man until the victim agreed to it. And he could be mighty persuasive.

I turned toward the alligator. It still hadn't moved. It still had its mouth wide open, its jagged teeth bared. I bladed off my shoulders toward the target and gripped the weapon with both hands, just like my dad taught me. Then I raised the gun up and assumed the modified Weaver shooter's stance.

I put the front sight on the animal's back, right between its front shoulders, where I figured its heart would be. If I was going to do this thing, I wanted to make sure my first shot was the kill shot.

"Come on, while we're young."

I frowned, but kept the weapon up. I breathed in, let it out, breathed in, let it out.

The gun jumped in my hands.

"Whoa!" Jeff said. "You nailed him!"

And I had. There was a jagged red hole right between his shoulder blades, exactly where I'd trained the weapon's front sight.

But it hadn't been the lethal shot I'd hoped for. He still lay there, his mouth wide open, staring at us with what I now believe to be dumb reptilian incomprehension, but to my fourteen-year-old brain seemed like a challenge. I think it was the challenge that pissed me off, that hardened me, because it was that precise moment that my nausea turned to anger.

"That son of a bitch is gonna die," I said, and fired again and again, until I'd burned through a box of fifty shells.

Then I handed the gun to Jeff and he did the same.

The whole time that alligator kept his mouth open, and the only movement he made was to swing his huge head from side to side, like he might be able to catch the bullets in his mouth.

Jeff and I laughed and cheered each other on until the alligator finally sagged to the ground and its blood-spattered mouth closed.

We laughed about it the whole way home, even though I felt sick inside. It didn't seem to bother Jeff though, so I put on a brave face and told myself there was no reason to feel sick about what we'd done. It was an alligator, after all. Who was going to miss an alligator? And I think I'd almost convinced myself of that as I put the weapon back into my father's gun cabinet and closed the door and turned around.

Only to see my father standing there…looking like I'd just spit on everything he believed in.

My dad had kicked my ass before, because I was no stranger to trouble, and I braced myself for more of the same.

Instead, he said: "Jeff, it's time for you to go home."

Jeff had muttered, "Yes, sir," and got out of there as fast as he could.

Then my dad just stared at me. I waited and waited for him to grab me and pull me out of the closet and beat my ass. But that didn't happen. He just stared at me.

Then he stepped into the closet and I braced myself for the worst.

But that didn't happen either.

He just held out his hand for the key and I gave it to him. He opened the safe and took out his service revolver and I watched him open the cylinder and visibly and physically check to ensure he had an unloaded weapon, just as he had instructed me to do every time we went shooting together. Then he put the weapon back into cabinet and closed and locked the door. He didn't speak.

Finally I couldn't take it anymore and I said, "Dad, look, I'm real–"

"Get out of here," he said.

"I'm sorry, I–"

"Get out."

"Are you grounding me?"

He wouldn't look at me, just stared at the gun cabinet. "I don't care where you go," he said through clenched teeth. "Just get out of here."

I'd been walking around on eggshells ever since, not sure where I was going. He hadn't said another word about it, but there'd been plenty of those moments like the one that passed between us on the front porch that morning as we watched Max fight the crawdad.

I would rather he just kicked my ass and be done with it, but that wasn't how my dad dealt with things.

That wasn't his style.

My dad was the kind of man who accumulated information and experiences, and took his time to come to a decision.

For the most part, his hesitation had resulted in a loving sort of forgiveness.

There were plenty of moments in our shared past that had been dotted with stupid things on my part. I knew that. I wasn't above admitting that I was a hard kid to manage.

My dad had been tested plenty of times before, and he'd always reacted the same way. He'd studied me. He'd stared at me until I eventually broke down and told him everything, terrified of that dead stare.

But that wasn't the father who stood before me now.

He looked perplexed. And yet, he looked profoundly angry.

Even though Jeff had been there with me, for most of it at least, I didn't feel comfortable talking with him about it. I'd seen my dad change before my very eyes. I'd seen him grow hard and mean and distant. I'd seen my dad turn into a man I didn't really understand.

Jeff, to be honest, wasn't much of a listener when it came to stuff like that, and anyway his advice was usually suspect.

So I didn't bother. I just bent my back into the oar and started paddling.

So did Jeff.

* * *

A few minutes later we were in the middle of the street in front of Mr. Moore's house. Mr. Moore was still in his little aluminum boat, over by his front porch, and his neighbors were all standing in their doorways, watching.

I could tell right away what Mr. Moore meant about the smell. As soon as the wind shifted and I caught a whiff of it my stomach seized up and I almost barfed.

"Oh God," I said.

From the front of the canoe, Jeff coughed, then turned his head my way and nodded.

"Not good," he said.

I didn't see my dad.

I was about to call out to Mr. Moore and ask after him when suddenly my dad lurched out of the shrimp boat's cabin, fumbled his way over to the gunwale, and puked his guts out into the water.

Nobody spoke. We just stood there, watching my dad wipe his lips with the back of his hand.

Finally, Mr. Moore said, "Wes…?"

My dad looked up. I saw him scan the crowd until he locked eyes on me. I swallowed the lump in my throat, expecting him to yell at me for being there.

Instead, he said, "Mark, go back home and get my police radio. Bring it to me right now."

"What is it, Dad?"

He closed his eyes, took a deep breath, and stood up as straight as he could on the slanting deck of the boat.

"Go, Mark. Men are dead in here. Now go."

I nodded, too freaked out to question him further.

"Hey Jeff, turn us around, okay?"
"Yeah," he said. "Yeah, okay."

* * *

We paddled back to my place as fast as we could go. Neither of us said anything about what we'd seen. But I think there was a sort of tacit communication that went between us, a vibe if you will, in which we agreed that we'd just started off on some kind of weird adventure. The storm and the flooding had been merely a prelude. But this, this was the meat of the play.

My mom tried to get us to slow down and tell her what was going on, but I just said that Dad needed us to get some things for him and went right back out the door. A few moments later we were slashing into the water with our paddles, going as fast as we could, totally ignoring the metal-on-metal grind of our canoe passing over our neighbors' cars.

Then we caught the smell again and we both stopped rowing.

I looked up.

The shrimp boat was about thirty feet away. My dad was standing on the gunwale near the stern, steadying himself with one hand on the rigging that had once held the boat's nets. That rigging was full of twigs and larger branches now. The sides of the boat were spackled with bright green leaves that the water had matted to the hull.

He had collected himself in the few minutes we were gone. He stood tall, and when he stared down at our approach he seemed strong and ready to act. He motioned for us to come closer. I stood up to hand him his radio and he knelt down to take it. In that moment–it lasted only seconds, but that was enough–I caught a glimpse over his shoulder at the open cabin door. I saw the walls there spattered with blood, and more blood pooling on the deck. A pale hand and a bit of wrist held the door ajar, and in the center of all that gore, staring at me with wide-open, terror-stricken eyes, was a severed head.

Bile rose up in my throat. It happened so fast I barely had time to choke it back down. I'd watched more horror movies than any other three kids at my school put together, and never once had I been grossed out to the point of puking. I don't know, maybe it was the smell. Whatever it was I had to close my eyes and force myself to get my act back under control.

When I opened them my dad was watching me.

"There are three bodies in there," he said. "At least as far as I can tell."

That surprised me. I'd expected him to tell me not to look. Instead, he was telling me about it. That had never happened before.

"All that blood from just three people?" I asked.

He nodded. "There's a lot of blood in the human body, Mark. One small person can bleed enough to cover an entire living room floor up to your shoe laces."

"Oh," I said. I stared again at that severed head, looked into its eyes. "Why…why is his head not with his body?"

My dad said nothing for a moment, just looked me in the eye. Finally he said, "It looks like they were eaten."

"What?"

"You heard me."

"Why would—an animal did that to them, right? Like an alligator, maybe?"

"I don't think so, Mark. I've seen enough bite marks to know what a human bite mark looks like. Those were made by a man."

"Oh God."

"Go home, Mark. Thanks for bringing me my radio. Go home and tell Mom I'm gonna be working for a bit. Tell her I'll start working on the house as soon as I can."

A pause.

"Hey, you hear me?"

I nodded. "Okay." I looked up at him. "What if…what if the man who did this comes back?"

He hesitated a moment before answering. "Rigor has set in. In this weather, in this heat, that means they were probably killed right about the time the storm was coming ashore. Still, I don't want you in this area until I tell you it's safe."

I nodded, but said nothing.

"Hey Mark?"

"Yeah, Dad."

"I love you, okay? This is bad, but you're okay. You understand that, don't you?"

"I…" I realized just then he had my shoulders in his hands, holding me like a little kid he was trying to examine for wounds. "I'm okay, Dad."

"Alright. You and Jeff go now."

I nodded again.

I sank down into the canoe and pulled the paddle to my chest.

"Jeff," my dad said, "you guys go back home."

I was too stunned to say anything. I just sat there with the paddle clutched to my chest as Jeff used *his* paddle to push us away from the boat. I had the sense of movement below me, but not of time passing. I just felt numb. And when at last I had enough presence of mind to turn around and look back, I saw my dad standing there, one hand on the rigging, the other half-raised in a mute salutation. I got the sense he was uncertain about what he'd just exposed me to.

I turned around, mechanically gripped my paddle, and started rowing home.

* * *

We stopped in the middle of the street, midway between my house and Jeff's.

"Hey Mark."

"Yeah?" I said.

"Dude, do you really want me to drop you off?"

"Huh?" I hadn't thought of anything else. I'd planned on going inside and hugging on Max while my mom made me breakfast.

"Let's go over and see if Alan and Eric are out."

"Jeff, I…"

"Hey."

I waited for him to say more, but he didn't. He was waiting for me to speak. "Hey, what?" I said.

"I'm just saying, you know, you don't have to go home."

"But I want to."

"Why? Because of what you saw?"

"Jeff, I saw a severed head. You have no idea how much blood…"

He hesitated for a moment, then he said: "Well, if that's what you want. But I just got to tell you, we're never gonna see something like this again."

"You said that before. We've had our fun. It doesn't feel like fun anymore."

"What are you gonna do, Mark? You gonna go inside and hang with your dog and your mom."

"Well, yeah, I guess."

"That and creep yourself out thinking about those bodies on that boat. Why not come with me? Take your mind off it."

I thought about that, and he did have a point. If I was going to be honest with myself I'd rather go cruising around with my friends than stay cooped up in the house with nothing but my dog and the memory of that head staring back at me from a pool of blood to keep me company.

"Okay," I said. "Alright."

"Now you're talking!" Jeff said.

* * *

Alan and Eric lived on Dunmoore Street, which was about four blocks north of Clearcrest, where Jeff and I lived. We found them at the neighborhood park. Clear Lake back then was all about NASA. Most of the kids we went to school with had a parent who worked there, like Jeff's dad for instance, who was an engineer for Grumman. It seemed everything in town, from the dry cleaners to the street names, had something to do with space exploration. Our neighborhood park was no different. The centerpiece of it was a forty-foot-high metal playscape made to look like a Saturn V rocket. It had a circular staircase on the inside and bars for walls so you could see out and a little room up in the nose cone where, three years earlier, I'd shared my first kiss with a girl named Lisa Rodriguez.

When we came up on them, Alan and Eric were in Alan's canoe watching a long black water moccasin glide through the lower level of the rocket.

Both turned to hail us and Eric said, "Can you believe this? This is totally badass."

"Yeah, it's pretty cool," Jeff said. "We found a dead body."

"Oh God," I muttered. Just like Jeff. Always had to steal the show.

It got the results he intended though.

Alan had nodded at us as we pulled up, but he'd gone right back to watching that water moccasin. He hated snakes. They gave him the willies, and I could tell he was watching that one to make sure it didn't decide to double back on them and try to get into the canoe. It wasn't a totally unreasonable fear as far as that goes. Water moccasins are mean. They'll do that to you, even when you're not doing anything to bother them. But of course as soon as he heard Jeff both he and Eric were staring at us.

"No way," Eric managed to say. He was still smiling, but the smile was slipping away fast.

"What are you talking about?" Alan asked.

"It was on the shrimp boat," Jeff said.

"Oh God," I said again.

Jeff was a master at keeping people on the hook like that. He said, "The storm surge carried a shrimp boat up from Kemah and smashed it into a pecan tree down at the end of our block. Mark's dad got called over to take a look at it because it smelled so bad and he found a dead body inside it. The guy was all torn up. You should have seen it. Mark's dad even puked his guts out. Right there in front of everybody. Just barfed over the side of the boat."

"No way," Eric said again. He and Alan both looked at me.

"It's true," I said. "But it was three bodies, actually. And my dad said it looked like they'd been eaten."

"What? No way." That one was from Alan. "Did he really puke?"

I nodded. "It was pretty sick. The smell was really bad."

"You saw the bodies?"

"I saw a head and a bunch of blood."

"Your dad let you onboard?" Alan asked. "Isn't that like a crime scene or something?"

I told them about handing my dad his radio and how I'd caught a glimpse of the scene over his shoulder. "I didn't touch anything," I added.

"But you smelled it, right?" Alan asked.

"Yeah." I looked over at Jeff. "We both did."

"It was so totally nasty," Jeff added, and laughed.

"It's not funny," Alan said. I thought he meant because somebody had died, but that wasn't it. "When you smell something," he explained, "you take a little part of that something inside you. Smells are particles, you know. You guys have got part of those dead men inside you now."

"Huh?" Jeff said, looking as confused as Alan and Eric had when he told them about the bodies.

Alan nodded. He was taller than the rest of us, with freckles across the bridge of his nose and a slender face that made him look more delicate than someone of his height should look. It didn't help that he wore clunky, black-framed glasses, either. It made him look like the poster boy for nerd camp. I was on the football team, and every once in a while one of the guys on the team would ask me why I was friends with someone who looked like such a dweeb. I always defended Alan whenever I could, but he didn't make it easy on me. He just had a knack for saying things that normal people knew better than to say.

Like now.

"The way you smell is your nose picks up small airborne particles of the thing making the scent. Little bits and pieces, if you will. They break off whatever's giving off the smell and it gets inside your nose, inside you, where your body and mind work together to decide if it's a good smell or a bad smell. Whether it's food or danger or whatever. You guys have got part of those dead bodies inside you now."

Jeff and I looked at each other. Neither of us was smiling now.

Jeff said, "That's not true, is it?"

Alan shrugged, a why-would-I-lie gesture.

"Oh God," I muttered. It was already getting hot, up in the high 80s, but I felt a little chill crawl over my skin just the same.

Then Eric slapped Alan in the shoulder. "Dude, way to be Debbie Downer." He turned to Jeff and me. "Hey, show us the shrimp boat."

I knew this was coming.

"No way," I said. "My dad told me to go home. He'd ground me for sure if he knew I didn't do as he said."

"I don't think that's all that likely," Alan said. "If he didn't ground you for stealing his gun, I doubt seriously he'd ground you for wanting to go exploring all this."

"Nice," Eric said. "Real nice."

"What?" Alan asked. "What did I say?"

"He's right, you know?" Jeff said.

"Who? Alan?" I asked.

"No, Eric. We could park a short ways off, out of the way of the action. Nobody'll notice us. You know the cops are gonna be bringing lots of boats and crime scene stuff and all that. It's gonna be a show, man."

That was true. I'd heard my dad tell stories about working major crime scenes, about how chaotic they could be. I could only imagine what it'd be like trying to do what they had to do from boats.

"Sure," I said, aware that Jeff had once again talked me out of my common sense and into defying my father, "let's go."

* * *

The four of us came together accidentally. I'd played on a Little League Baseball team with Eric years before, when we were like five, so I knew him that way. But we went to a big elementary school and because none of us had any of the same classes, we recognized each other but didn't know each other.

Then, about three years ago, about the same time I was sharing my first kiss with Lisa Rodriguez in the nose cone of the Rocket, my parents bought the house on Clearcrest, across the street from Jeff's family. Jeff and I started hanging out together, and quickly became good friends.

I played defensive end for the football team, and he played clarinet in the band. His family was really into church; mine had never set foot in one. I liked Marvel; he liked DC. We should have been natural enemies, or at least given each other a disdainfully wide berth, but we just got on great. Or, as my dad sometimes said, like a house on fire.

Jeff told me he hung out with two other guys who lived a few blocks over. I knew Eric from before, so that was an easy fit. And even Alan, with his big black-framed glasses and his knack for always saying the worst thing he could possibly say, was kind of a known element. His older sister, Heather Crawford, had been my babysitter for a while, and though I'd never talked with him until Jeff introduced us, I'd heard plenty of stories from Heather about her nerdy little brother. And he was cool, like I said, in his own way.

So our little gang came together.

* * *

We turned our canoes toward the end of Dunmoore, Eric and Alan's street, where it connected with Brook Forest Blvd. From there it was a quick ride up to Clearcrest, where the shrimp boat waited in Mr. Moore's pecan tree. Eric was drilling me with questions about the severed head I'd seen when I caught a flash of movement and heard something thunk into the side of Alan and Eric's canoe. A moment later, a rock landed in our canoe and bounced around in the well between Jeff and me, eventually settling at our feet.

"What the hell?" Jeff said.

I looked at the rock, looked at Jeff, and then looked toward the line of houses off to our left.

"What happened?" Alan asked.

We saw them then, Billy Steyn and Matt Drake and Lee Johnson. They were standing behind some bushes on a dry patch of grass about forty feet away, and at that point there was no doubt about what had happened. They'd collected an impressive mound of rocks, almost like they'd been expecting us. As we were caught out in the middle of the street, with nothing to use for cover and the current running strong against us, it seemed like they'd chosen the perfect place from which to ambush us. No matter which direction we went it would take us several minutes to get to cover, so we were sitting ducks.

The air filled with stones.

Billy Steyn and his friends had been picking on us for about two years at that point. We got on their radar because of these homemade nunchucks Jeff made. One morning, Jeff and I and a couple of other kids from our block were waiting for the bus to take us to school–under the pecan tree in Mr. Moore's front yard, in fact. We'd watched *Enter the Dragon* the night before and Jeff started swinging his nunchucks around like he was Bruce Lee. He even did a pretty fair imitation of those little chirpy noises that made Bruce Lee so much fun to watch. The next thing we knew Billy Steyn, who was a sophomore but already had his license, skidded his ratty old blue Buick up to the curb next to us. He and Lee climbed out, Iron Maiden's "Run to the Hills" still blaring from their radio, and yanked the nunchucks out of Jeff's hand.

Jeff was too surprised to put up a fight. He just looked at me and shrugged.

There must have been nine of us 6th and 7th graders standing around then, and none of us knew what to do. Billy and Lee were both sixteen, and outweighed every kid at that bus stop by an easy thirty pounds, and nearly all of that in muscle.

Billy and Lee looked around like they expected at least one of us to put up a challenge, but when none of us did they just laughed and got back in their car.

I came to my senses then.

Or perhaps I didn't.

Maybe I exposed some fatal flaw in my genetic engineering, a predisposition to self-destructive behavior.

Either way, it doesn't matter. I spit a big loogie on the back fender of Billy Steyn's crappy old Buick and called them both assholes.

Even gave them the bird with both hands.

The results were predictable. I should have been able to predict them, at any rate. Instead I thought merely of my pride. I was still thinking of things like honor when the two of them jumped out of the car, threw me down, and proceeded to beat my ass six ways to Sunday.

I went to school that day a mangled wreck: but strangely, with more pride than ever before.

But I'd also managed to put myself squarely in Billy's crosshairs. The Circle K down by the elementary school had a little arcade in it–Galaga; Tempest; Centipede; Asteroids; Defender–and every time he'd catch me and the rest of my friends down there he'd mess with the controls to make us die and then maybe play a few games himself using the quarters we'd lined up along the rails at the base of the monitor.

Once I was on my bike–I rode a Mongoose BMX back then–going over to see Alan and Eric, when Billy and the rest of his gang drove up behind and threw a beer bottle at me. It missed and bounced off the front tire of my bike.

I think it made them mad I didn't crash because they stopped right in front of me and made me stop.

Billy got out and grabbed my handlebars and dumped my bike over, spilling me into the curb.

Satisfied, he drove away.

Another time, and I have no idea what he was doing at my intermediate school, he was walking the upstairs hallway and saw me. I'd been in Mrs. Durham's health class at the time, and she'd sent me out to the hallway because I'd made her mad, again. Mrs. Durham was easily the cruelest, nastiest, most wrinkled old bitch at Clear Lake Intermediate School, and I made her mad pretty much on a daily basis. But this time, it made me a sitting duck. Billy pushed me up against the lockers and asked if I wanted to spit any more loogies. When I didn't answer he spun me around, grabbed the hair on the back of my head, and smashed my face into the lockers.

He didn't leave a mark but there'd been about thirty seconds when I couldn't breathe. When Mrs. Durham finally came out to the hall to tell me I could come back to class my hair was a mess and my eyes were red from crying and Billy was of course long gone.

It went that way every time he saw me.

Now was no different.

The hail of rocks continued.

The three of them were throwing stones as fast as they could pick them up, and all we could do was swat them away with our paddles.

I hit a few, but that did little good.

Jeff caught one in the cheek and the rock that hit him landed in the well of our canoe. He dropped his paddle into the water and put a hand up to the wound.

"Get the paddle," I said. "Dude, don't let it go."

I stopped paddling, and we drifted back in the direction we'd come, floating even with the paddle.

"Grab it," I said.

"Am I bleeding?" he asked.

It was just a bruise, no blood. "You're fine," I said. "Get your paddle. We need to get out of here."

Just then I heard Eric cry out. I turned their way and saw him cradling his face in his hands, his fingers red with fresh blood. More rocks hit their canoe and Alan pulled his paddle close and curled into a fetal ball in the belly of his canoe.

The rocks kept coming.

For a moment I thought: Get out of the canoe; flip it over and use it as a turtle does its shell.

But then I got pissed. My dad told me once that he became a cop because he wanted to make sure the working man got the justice he worked so hard to deserve. He said bullies defined the world, and if he could do his little part in his little corner of the world to change that, he would consider his life well spent.

That impressed me when he'd said it, and it impressed me still, as I entered my teenage years. Most of our interactions just ended with me being pissed off, but that thing he said mattered.

It still mattered.

Bullies deserved to get it shoved back in their face.

In many ways, those few words from my father were my inspiration, the source of my courage.

Mad as I was, hurt as I was, I picked up the rock that had bruised Jeff's cheek and I threw it toward our hated Gang of Three.

I'll tell you now I do not believe in divine providence. Or karma. Or any of that other religious nonsense. My dad had no problem whatsoever bending his head whenever someone called for a prayer, but my mom was different. She was the only person I'd ever met who would regularly sneer at a church as we passed it by in the car. When someone randomly called for a prayer, I noticed she never bent her head. I thought that courageous, and honest, and I did the same, whenever I could.

But back to the rock.

I can only tell you that I heaved that rock with everything I had. Billy just happened to come around the side of the house at just the right moment. He was looking the other way at just the right moment. He caught my rock right in the forehead and never saw it coming. Though I was forty feet away I heard the crack of stone on bone plain as day. He sagged to his knees and put his hands over his face and when he took them away to yell at me he had runners of blood coming down his face.

"You're dead, Eckert! You hear me? I'm gonna kill you! I am going to beat your ass into the dirt!"

I caught Alan and Eric staring at me, both of them frozen in fear. We'd seen Billy mad before, but never like this.

"Go suck it, Billy," I yelled. "I hope I gave you a concussion!"

"Oh Jesus," Alan said.

Beside me, Jeff sat up and said: "Mark, what are you doing?"

I ignored him. "You hear me, Billy? I hope it hurts, you stupid son of a bitch. I hope it hurts bad! Go on and cry about it, little girl!"

"Man, you're dead," Billy said. "Get him!"

He and Lee and Matt charged into the water.

Alan said: "Mark, what do we do?"

"Oh crap," I muttered. I picked up my paddle and motioned for the others to do the same. "Go with the current," I said. "Let's go, let's go!"

We'd been fighting the current, but now we turned back in the direction from which we'd come and beat the water for all we were worth. Billy and his gang gained on us for a moment, and Billy even got to within a finger's length from our canoe, but once we got going we managed to create some distance between us; and when I looked back Billy and the others were standing hip-deep in the water, staring death rays into our backs.

"You're dead," Billy yelled after us. His face was still bleeding. "You hear me? You're dead, Eckert."

"Yeah?" I yelled back. "Looks like you're the one who's bleeding."

"Dude," Jeff said, "don't make it worse."

"Yeah," Alan said. "He's gonna beat your ass."

"Yeah?" I said. I was pissed. But more than that, I was sick of running. "So what? Let him do what he's gonna do. I'm sick of his crap. I'm sick of being bullied."

I turned to Billy.

"You hear me, Billy? I hope it hurts!"

Nobody had an answer for that.

I thought of George C. Scott in *Patton*, that scene where he's standing on the cliff, looking down at his tanks thoroughly routing Rommel. "I beat you! I beat you, you son of a bitch," he'd said. "I beat you because I read your book!"

I loved that from the moment I first heard it, sitting next to my dad on our couch with a big thing of Jiffy Pop between us.

Now I was living it.

There's something to be said about getting under your enemy's skin.

* * *

I got home in time for dinner.

My mom had lit a bunch of candles and the inside of the house glowed with a warm, soothing orange light. She was sitting at the kitchen table, reading one of her medical journals, when I walked in the back door. On the island was a platter of raw, cut up vegetables and some raw chicken marinating in soy sauce and honey in a Tupperware tub.

"Are we having fondue for dinner?" I asked.

She looked up from her reading and I could see she wasn't happy. "Where have you been? Where's your father?"

"Well, I was out with Jeff. We took his canoe down to the park. Dad must still be down at Mr. Moore's house."

"Your dog has been whining by the back door since you left."

A sense of relief welled up inside me. If she was trying to play the dog-missed-you-guilt-trip on me, clearly she wasn't that mad.

I looked over at the corner where Max was sprawled out on the floor. He had perked his head when I entered, but hadn't bothered to come over and greet me. He was watching me, his eyes sad and reproachful.

"Hey Max," I said. "Want a Milkbone?"

"I've already given him plenty today," my mom said, too late. He jumped up and trotted over to the refrigerator, eager for his snack.

"Fine. Go ahead," my Mom said. "When your dad asks why his dog is so fat you'll be the one to answer for it."

I got Max his biscuit and scratched his ears while he wolfed it down.

"I thought you said you were going to help him."

"Huh?" I said.

"Your father," my mom said. "I thought you said you were going to help him."

"Well, I did. I brought him his police radio."

"What for?"

I paused before I answered, wondering how much to tell her of what I'd seen. It wasn't much of a decision to make, though. What I didn't tell her Dad would as soon as he got home, and if she knew he was doing his police thing I figured she wouldn't be mad at him for being out of the house all day. So I laid it all out for her, everything I knew.

"You're not joking, are you?"

"No, Mom, I swear. That's what I saw."

"That's horrible."

I thought about that severed head and I had to agree. It was horrible.

Just then my dad came in through the front door. Max raised his ears, barked once, and went running for the door.

"We're in the kitchen," my mom said, calling out to him.

He came in with Max and sat down at the table next to my mom. He was dripping wet and filthy, and he looked exhausted.

"Is it true what Mark said?" Mom asked. "Were those bodies really…eaten?"

He nodded.

"How does that happen?"

He shrugged. "There are some sick people in this world. Ten years ago it was that Dean Corll guy who killed all those kids in the 2nd Ward. Five years ago Jim Jones and all those wackos down in Jonestown killed themselves. Now we've got some lunatic running around eating people. It's a crazy world."

"Are we safe here, Wes?"

He took a moment to answer her. His eyes were bloodshot; his face caked with grime and grease. For the first time I realized that his hair was starting to turn gray at the temples. Then he reached out and took my mom's hands in his.

"We're gonna be fine," he said.

"You promise, Wes."

"Yeah," he said. He suddenly sounded breezy, like this was no big deal, though I thought maybe he was just putting on an act for my mother's benefit. "Yeah, I promise."

* * *

After dinner my dad and I went around prying the boards off the windows. Then my mom gave us each a bucket of soapy water and a sponge and sent us off to our respective showers to get cleaned up. When I was clean I took a bag of Twizzlers up to my room and lit a candle and read *Tarzan of the Apes* until I drifted off to sleep.

I had thought the horrors of the day were behind me. The severed head; the rock fight with Billy; my hometown under water: I thought I'd wake up and it would all be in the past, just some cool memory in an otherwise boring summer.

But as I read about Tarzan's battles with Kerchak, a real battle, and one far more savage, was raging down the street.

The real horror of that summer was just beginning.

* * *

The next morning I woke to the doorbell.

Tired and stiff from rowing all the previous day I went to the landing at the top of the stairs and watched my dad as he opened the front door.

A man in jeans and a green t-shirt was standing there. He had a gun and a badge on his hip and he clearly knew my dad because they called each other by their first names. I guessed this was Detective Gene Travis, whom my dad had mentioned the night before. I'd asked him what happened to the shrimp boat and my dad had said that a detective named Gene Travis had arranged for it to be towed back to dry land so that it could be put on a truck and sent to the Harris County Crime Lab for testing.

"We got us a bit of a problem," Gene Travis said.

"What kind of problem?" my dad answered.

"That guy down there, the one who reported the boat to you…"

"Yeah, Tom Moore."

"Yeah. I went over there this morning to get his statement and, well, I'm sorry if he was a good friend of yours, but he's dead. He and his wife both."

"What?"

"They were all tore up, Wes. Same as those bodies you found on that shrimp boat. He and his wife, it looks like they've been eaten."

My dad didn't say anything to that.

"I think it's pretty plain whoever did this is the same person who killed those men on the boat," Detective Travis said. "He must have stayed in the area after the boat crashed."

"I looked all over that scene," my dad said. "I didn't see anybody suspicious. Believe me, I looked."

"We did too. We searched the area top to bottom. He must have gotten inside the house when Tom Moore was outside with you. Or maybe before you got there."

"Must have been before I got there. Gene, I looked all over."

"Okay, well, I'm sorry again."

"Yeah. Yeah, thanks."

Gene Travis left and my dad closed the door. A moment later he said, "Mark, you heard that?"

Oh crap, I thought. He knows I'm here. How did he know I was here?

"Yes, sir," I said.

"Come down."

I did. I said, "Dad, how are they gonna figure out who did this?"

"They'll start with the boat. It had to have come from somewhere. They'll figure out where, then they'll look into calls that came in just before the storm. They might get lucky and find a suspicious person call. Maybe somebody even made an arrest. That'd give them a name, or at least a description. If that doesn't work, they'll get into the forensics, see if they can find prints and stuff like that."

"Oh," I said. That seemed reasonable. Police work always sounded simple the way he described it.

"Do you know why I let you listen to that?"

"Um, no, not really. I didn't think you knew I was there."

"You're congested and you were breathing through your nose. I could hear the breath whistling in your nose."

"Oh."

"Breathe through your mouth if you need to be quiet." He crossed his arms over his chest and studied me. "It's gonna take them a while to figure this out. Certainly a few days, maybe longer. I let you listen in on that because I wanted you to hear that this is serious. This isn't a game. You listen to me, and you do as I say. You be careful when you're out. You screwed up when you took my gun out, and I'm still pissed about that. Don't be stupid like that again. You hear me?"

"Yes sir," I said. "I hear you."

* * *

The floodwaters didn't stick around long.

By midday nearly all the cars and trucks that had been parked in the street were visible, just the tires still below the surface. The crawdads were gone too. The phones and the electricity and the water were all still out, but the flood was going away. I think my little corner of the neighborhood was the last to stay flooded because we were right next to the greenbelt, but even down where we lived you could tell the water was going away. It left behind a sour, sewage smell.

I went out to the front yard and watched the commotion down at Mr. Moore's house. There were two Harris County Sheriff's cars down there, and a big 18-wheeler flatbed with a crane to get rid of the shrimp boat. The deputies had come by and asked my dad to help out and of course he'd gone down there. Jeff joined me and together we watched them load the boat onto the truck and drive it away.

"Is it true about Mr. Moore?" he asked.

I told him it was. "His wife too."

"My mom is totally freaking out."

"Mine too."

"What does your dad think?"

"He said the guy must have been hiding inside Mr. Moore's house. He was probably waiting for all the commotion to die down."

"Yeah, but he ate them. What kind of lunatic does that?"

"I don't know," I admitted. "It's pretty screwed up."

"You know what Eric said?"

"No, what?"

"He said it was Dean Corll. He said the Candy Man's back."

"That's ridiculous. Dean Corll's dead."

"I'm just telling you what he said. I told him the same thing, that Corll was dead, but you know him. He said the Houston Police Department faked his death to keep the public off their backs."

Dean Corll was about as close to a boogeyman as we had. Ten years earlier he'd gone on a killing spree. With the help of two teenage helpers, who earned $200 a head for the boys they lured into Corll's grasp, he'd kidnapped, raped, tortured and murdered a total of twenty-seven teenage boys from some of the poorest neighborhoods in Houston's 2nd Ward. People in his neighborhood called him the Candy Man because he was famous for passing out free candy to the kids. He was eventually murdered by one of his teenage helpers, which put his spree to an end, but did nothing to assuage the fear he left in his wake.

My dad had never really talked about Corll, not to me anyway, but I knew that the Houston Police Department took a real beating in the court of public opinion over what became known as the Houston Mass Murders. So many children had gone missing from the same neighborhood, but there'd been no concentrated effort to look into the disappearances. I guess conspiracy theories about the Candy Man coming back from the grave were inevitable.

"I don't believe that," I said. "Do you?"

"No."

"Corll's dead," I said. I meant to give it a note of finality, of authority, but for whatever reason that assured tone was missing.

* * *

Later, we went over to Alan's house and played Monopoly.

It didn't take Eric long to bring up Dean Corll. "You don't think it's possible the Houston Police Department faked his death?"

"No, I don't," I said.

"Why not?"

"Because it was all over the news. They had a trial and everything. You don't really think they'd have all of that if they faked his death, do you?"

"I don't know. I guess it's possible."

"It's not."

"Well what about those two guys who helped him? Maybe it's one of them."

Dean Corll had enlisted two teenage boys, Elmer Wayne Henley and David Brooks, to help lure in his victims. The boys earned $200 a head for each victim and even helped in the tortures and murders and the disposal of the bodies. Both were serving life sentences for their part in the killings and I told Eric as much.

"Well, maybe they escaped."

"Oh jeez," I said. "I'm done. I'm not gonna debate conspiracy theories with you."

"I'm just asking questions," Eric said.

"You're being stupid," I said. I'd had enough. "Hey Alan, you mind if I get another Coke?"

"Sure," he said. "Help yourself."

"Thanks."

I went downstairs to his kitchen. His mom had put out a cooler filled with ice and cokes. I opened a can of Sprite and was throwing away the pop-top when Alan's older sister Heather came in the back door.

Back when she was my babysitter she had been a little on the heavy side. Not fat, but definitely chunky. And, really, at the time, I hadn't been old enough to think of her as a girl. She was just the person my parents hired to watch me when they wanted to go for dinner and a movie. I liked her. I liked her a lot. But I was too young to see her as a *girl*. You know, in a sexual way.

She was definitely more than that now. Her freshman year at the University of Texas had been good to her. She was slim and toned and with her hair teased up and her blouse hanging off her shoulder, she was, I'll be honest here, kind of a fox.

I think she knew it, too.

Girls have to know it, when they look delicious.

I said, "Back from school, huh?" I tried to make it sound cool but my voice cracked.

I'm sure she noticed, but she didn't let on. Despite the change in her appearance, she was still genuine. She was still kind.

"Yeah, my parents are bugging me to find a job."

"Ah," I said. I leaned up against the counter and took a swig of my Sprite. She really did look good. I was crazy about that off-the-shoulder look some of the girls wore, and she rocked it.

"How are your mom and dad?" she asked.

"They're good. They're working a lot."

"I'm gonna have to drop your mom a line here pretty soon. I really appreciate her writing that letter of recommendation for me."

"Yeah, come by," I said. "I know they'd love to see you."

She nodded, and it felt like we'd pretty much dried up our topics for conversation. Back when she was my babysitter we'd talk for hours. I used to love hanging out with her. But now, with her being in college and me still just a kid, it felt there was a real gulf between us, like we didn't have anything in common anymore. It made me feel kind of depressed.

But then she said, "I heard about the rock fight."

"Oh yeah?"

"Yeah. You really hit Billy in the face?"

I laughed. "Yeah."

"I would have paid five dollars to see that. That guy is such a dick."

I laughed again. "It was pretty cool."

"I bet it was." She smiled. But then she grew serious. "Listen, you need to be careful with him. He's a first rate jerk, but he's dangerous. I know girls that have gone out with him. He's mean. He likes to hurt girls. Do you know what I mean when I say hurt?"

I waved that away like I wasn't worried. "He doesn't scare me."

"Mark, I'm being serious. You need to be careful. You'll do that, won't you? You'll be careful around him?"

"Yeah," I said. I was a little surprised by how stern she suddenly seemed, like she was my babysitter all over again, but an adult this time. "Sure. I'll be careful."

"Good. Say hi to your mom for me."

"Yeah, I will."

She nodded and went up to her room.

* * *

That night, because I'd been spending so much time in canoes of late, I read Algernon Blackwood's "The Willows" before drifting off to bed. When I woke the next morning the floodwater was gone from the street and the long process of cleaning up trash and busted tree limbs began. Mom had to get back to her practice, so Dad and I got busy with the yard. The pecan tree in our front yard hadn't done very well in the storm, and several of its heaviest branches had broken away. Those we cut up with a chainsaw and loaded into the back of my dad's pickup. It was hard work and we didn't stop for a break until about one.

We were in the kitchen, eating peanut butter and jelly sandwiches and drinking warm Cokes when there was a knock at the door.

"I'll get it," I said.

It was Detective Gene Travis again. He looked grim. He was dressed in a suit, but his shoes were muddy. And he was carrying a thick accordion file stuffed with papers and pictures.

"My dad's in the kitchen," I said. "You can come in if you want."

"No thanks. I got all this mud on my shoes. Could you ask your dad to come out here, please?"

"Yes, sir."

I turned toward the kitchen. "Hey Dad!"

My dad came around the corner and he stiffened as soon as he saw Gene Travis. "What is it?" he asked.

Detective Travis looked at me and then at my father.

"Mark, go on," my dad said. "I need to talk to this detective for a bit."

I opened my mouth to object, but stopped myself before a single word came out. There wouldn't have been any point.

Instead I sighed and shuffled back towards the kitchen. Maybe they didn't know I was listening, but I was.

"There were two more last night," Travis said.

"Oh no," my dad said. "I saw the mud on your shoes. I figured something was up."

"Yeah."

"Who was it? Do you know?"

"Two college girls, a couple streets over."

I was standing near the back door, but that froze me in place. Max was waiting on the other side, watching me through the glass, no doubt wondering why I was just standing there. He let out a bark, but I didn't move.

And then Gene Travis said the name I'd been praying he wouldn't say, and my blood went cold.

Heather Crawford was dead.

* * *

What I remember most of that moment, the moment after Gene Travis left and my dad stood there by the front door, was him walking into my mom's office and picking up the phone–to call my mom, I guess–and finding the thing inoperative.

I remember him slamming the phone back down on the cradle and muttering something to himself and then sitting there, in her chair, with his face in his hands.

That was all.

Of my own pain, I have no memory.

* * *

Later, my mom made it home.

Dad hadn't said a word to me. I'd been sitting on the stairs, waiting for something, anything, from him. But I'd gotten nothing.

When my mom got home, Dad wasted little time.

He pulled her aside and whispered what he'd learned from Detective Travis.

What I remember is my mom going into her office and dropping into her chair and then crying like I'd never seen her cry before.

I wanted to go to her. I wanted to say something that would *mean* something. But listening to her cry I knew I just wasn't up for it. Whatever it was she needed to hear was a mystery to me.

Hell, my own feelings were a mystery to me.

The only thing I knew was that a great big crater had just been punched into the center of my world.

* * *

My dad worked the overnight shift, and usually by the time my mom came home from her practice, he was about to walk out the door.

"You're going to work?" she asked, like she couldn't believe it.

"I have to. Now that the roads are open I have to go in to work. I expect my guys to come in to work. I can't very well skip out when I'm telling them they have to."

"But now? Wes, I…I need you here."

I was listening to this exchange from my perch at the top of the stairs, and this time, I was breathing in and out through my mouth, so as not to be overheard.

"I'm hurting too," my dad said. I was surprised by the tenderness I heard there. He sounded vulnerable. He never sounded vulnerable.

"Oh Wes, why do you have to go?"

And then, strangely, his tone hardened. "Come on, Meredith. You married a cop. You knew what you were getting. I love you. But I have to go."

"But you don't need to."

"What are you talking about?"

"Wes, I make enough you don't have to do that anymore. You could retire today, if you wanted. I could finance that dog training school you've always wanted to start. This is the perfect neighborhood for it. We could do all of that today, if you wanted."

"You want me to stop being a cop? Is that what you're saying?"

"No," she said. "Wes, I want you to be happy. I want *us* to be happy."

"Aren't we? Are you saying you're not happy?"

"Wes, no. Please. Please don't make this a battle."

"A battle? What the hell, Meredith? I'm not fighting with you."

"No, I know that. I'm sorry. I didn't mean…I just…I just want you to hear me on this. I love you, Wes."

"What else have I been doing? That's all I've been doing is hearing you. I hear you say you want us to be happy. That means you're *not* happy right now. Right? Am I right? I mean, what the hell? You know what kind of hours I work."

"But Wes, I never see you. Our schedules are so messed up. All I want to do is spend time with you, like we used to do. Please, let's be together on this."

A pause. An awful pause.

"Ah Christ, get out of the way. I'm going to work."

I saw my dad storm through the entryway at the foot of the stairs. I heard him yell, "Max, come!" and then the crash of muscle against metal as Max erupted from his crate and ran after my dad.

The door slammed.

For a moment, there was silence.

Then, filling that void, came my mother's sobbing.

* * *

It was a lovely evening. A warm, balmy dusk witnessed a darkness slowly pooling beneath the trees, and the slow rise of a yellow moon that was no longer full. I remember sitting before my open window, watching that moon, transfixed by its ancient mysteries.

I tried to read *The Hound of the Baskervilles*, but found Doyle's stilted 19th Century dialogue and shopworn formulae a bit tedious for such a night. After all, I'd just witnessed a confusing mix of emotions. The girl I'd known as both surrogate elder sister and latter day sex goddess was dead. It was Norma Jean Baker and Marilyn Monroe found dead in the nude on her bathroom floor. It was all the wonders of life and beauty stripped bare and laid low. No matter how I tried to process that, I came up with questions I couldn't answer.

On top of all that, my parents were fighting about things that didn't seem to make sense.

I put on a pair of jeans and went downstairs. My dad would be out all night. If his shift ended on time, which it rarely did, he'd be coming home about the time I was waking up for breakfast. So the house was quiet as I went downstairs. I went to the kitchen and poured myself a glass of water and drank it in the moonlight that filtered through the windows.

Only then did I hear my mother sobbing.

It was faint, but it was definitely her.

I walked down the main hallway, past the hall closet where we'd taken shelter the night of the storm, and reached the doorway to my parents' bedroom.

My mom was sitting on the edge of the bed, head bent low, chest hitching now and then with her sobbing.

"Mom, you okay?"

She swallowed as she looked up. She'd been crying a while, I could tell. Her face was red and puffy, her eyes bloodshot.

She raised her arms up and clutched her hands together in a *come here I need a hug* motion.

I went to her.

With her arms around me she said: "I can't believe she's dead."

"Me either."

"Are you okay?"

"I..." I started to say: *Sure, I'm fine;* even though I knew I wasn't. It was only then that I realized she wasn't really asking if *I* was okay, but if *we* were okay, if *we* could endure this together, she and I. "It hurts, Mom," I said. "I miss her."

"I know. I feel so ashamed."

"Ashamed?"

"That Hannett girl. She lived, but Heather died. I can't believe I wanted them to trade places. God, I feel so ashamed."

There was a survivor?

This was the first I'd heard of it. Clearly Dad had told her more than I'd overheard.

"Me too," I said.

My mom tightened her grip around me, and as she held me I could feel her body spasm and hitch with the flow of her tears. I endured it, though I was already focused in a different direction.

I'd remembered that huge accordion file Detective Travis had passed to my dad. He wouldn't have it with him tonight. He'd know better than that. His work on a Friday night was constant. He'd spend more time out of his vehicle, looking for some piece of crap burglar or wife beater who had just run from some young go-getter officer, than studying the slightly foreign notes of a partner police agency.

But I had the time.

And I had the file.

To my mom I said: "This has got me all turned around. I'm gonna go to bed. Are you gonna be okay?"

She nodded right before she let me go.

Then she said: "This is one of those dreadful moments you remember your whole life."

I had thought I'd be the one to walk away, but she left me then, standing there stunned by the awful truth of what she'd just said.

* * *

I went into my dad's office and looked around on his desk. He liked to smoke cigars, and occasionally I'd sneak a few from his humidor. That humidor was on the corner of the desk, next to a legal pad of notes for the midyear performance evaluations he was going to have to do on his troops–his "guys," as he called them.

But the file Detective Travis had given him wasn't there.

The drawers were noisy when opened, which is why I usually didn't go through his desk when one of my parents was home. But I really wanted that file, so I held my breath and, working very slowly, pulled one drawer after another open. I found it in the bottom right drawer, which in hindsight is where I should have looked at the start. It was the drawer I went to most often when I had the house to myself, for it was in that drawer that my dad kept his June 1980 issue of *Playboy*, featuring the first of many pictorials of Ola Ray, who would, a few years later, go on to become Michael Jackson's unsuspecting date in the "Thriller" video. I remember my first encounter with this magazine. I happened upon Ola Ray's centerfold–turned right to it would be another way of putting it–and found myself immediately struck by both the innocent and vulnerable beauty in her eyes and the exotically wonderful strangeness of her black skin. This being my first opportunity to look long and contemplatively upon the divine design of the naked, mature female form, I stared and studied in rapt fascination. I was smitten enough by her beauty to show the magazine to Jeff one day, and was rather taken aback by his comment: "Dude, your dad likes the dark meat."

This took what I had intended as a cool moment of sharing something awesome with my best friend to the first indication that perhaps we weren't to be lifetime friends. That distressed me, even if it didn't exactly anger me.

At the moment I had other fish to fry. I tossed the Ola Ray debut issue aside and took out the accordion file Detective Ward had left for my dad.

Who was this Hannett girl my mom was so ashamed of having wished dead?

I pulled out the file, which contained a large number of typewritten pages and even a few Polaroids of a girl in a party dress who had been ripped to shreds, and set it on the desk.

Then I started reading.

* * *

Rebecca–who preferred to be called Becca–Hannett had gone out that night with her friends, Heather Crawford and Jennifer Cowls. All three were high school friends home for the summer from the University of Texas at Austin, a school that *Playboy* magazine had once described as "not having an ugly girl on campus." I thought that a conspicuous instance of hyperbole when I read it in the aforementioned Ola Ray debut issue, but at the same time I had most sincerely hoped that it was true…for I planned to be there in just a few short years. And even the Becca Hannett portrayed in the Polaroids spread out before me, disheveled and dirty and tattered and seemingly vacant behind her two-thousand-yard stare that she was, was still obviously a good-looking girl. Long brown hair; a slender, almond-shaped face; perfect teeth: she was the kind of girl one followed with the eyes when she passed by, just to see if the backside was as good as the front.

It only took a few words of her statement to put those thoughts out of my mind, though. The girl, it was plain, had been through hell.

This is what I read of her interview with Detective Gene Travis:

DETECTIVE TRAVIS: Hi, Rebecca. I'm Detective Travis with the Harris County Sheriff's Office. Had a pretty bad scare tonight, huh?

DETECTIVE TRAVIS: Rebecca?

REBECCA HANNETT: I…I go by Becca.

DETECTIVE TRAVIS: Okay, Becca. That's good. Can we talk for a little bit about what happened tonight?

DETECTIVE TRAVIS: Becca, I see you nodding your head. But can you say the words for me, please? Is it okay if we talk about what happened?

REBECCA HANNETT: Yes.

DETECTIVE TRAVIS: I see you're dressed up. You were going out tonight?

DETECTIVE TRAVIS: Becca, please, don't just nod. I need you to answer me.

REBECCA HANNETT: Yes.

DETECTIVE TRAVIS: Okay, good. You were with some friends, weren't you?

REBECCA HANNETT: Yes.

DETECTIVE TRAVIS: Who were they?

REBECCA HANNETT: Heather Crawford and Jennifer Cowls.

DETECTIVE TRAVIS: Friends of yours from school?

DETECTIVE TRAVIS: Becca, don't just nod. Were these girls friends of yours from school?

REBECCA HANNETT: Yes.

DETECTIVE TRAVIS: How long have you known them?

REBECCA HANNETT: Since we were kids. I don't know, 2nd grade maybe. We go to UT Austin now. I'm sorry. We…oh god.

DETECTIVE TRAVIS: Becca, I know this is hard. This won't take long. Tell me please what happened tonight.

REBECCA TRAVIS: This is our summer vacation. Heather was supposed to be getting a job and my parents wanted me to do the same. We figured we had a week or two at most to hang out and party. We wanted to go dancing, you know, up in the gay bars in Westheimer?

DETECTIVE TRAVIS: Yes. Who was driving?

REBECCA HANNETT: I was. I picked up Jennifer–she had crabbed a bottle of vodka from her mom's liquor cabinet–and then we went over to pick up Heather.

DETECTIVE TRAVIS: Had Jennifer opened the vodka?

DETECTIVE TRAVIS: Becca, don't just shake your head please.

REBECCA HANNETT: No.

DETECTIVE TRAVIS: Okay, so the two of you have driven from her house over to Heather Crawford's house. What happened next?

REBECCA HANNETT: He killed them.

DETECTIVE TRAVIS: Who did? Who killed who?

REBECCA HANNETT: That gross guy. That hairy guy.

DETECTIVE TRAVIS: Hairy, what do you mean?

REBECCA HANNETT: He was all hairy. I don't know. He was gross.

DETECTIVE TRAVIS: Becca, tell me what you mean. How was he all hairy?

REBECCA HANNETT: I don't know. He had...a big beard and hair that was all over the place. He had hair on his chest and on his arms and he...he was naked. He was gross. God, and he growled...oh god, he sounded like a mean dog or something. Oh god.

DETECTIVE TRAVIS: Tell me what happened, Becca? You guys have just gone to pick up Heather...

REBECCA HANNETT: Yes. We were walking back to the car. I was standing on the driver's side, trying to get the keys in the door lock. It was dark and I was having trouble. Heather and Jennifer were laughing, they were talking about this guy Jennifer knew back at school who...

DETECTIVE TRAVIS: Becca, you okay?

DETECTIVE TRAVIS: Becca, I can see you shaking your head. I know this hard. But if we're going to catch this guy, I need you to be strong. Now, you're standing next to your car, it's dark, what then?

REBECCA HANNETT: He killed them.

DETECTIVE TRAVIS: Okay. Tell me about that.

REBECCA HANNETT: I was trying to get my keys in the lock. Heather and Jennifer were talking. And then we heard him in the shrubs at the edge of Heather's front yard.

DETECTIVE TRAVIS: Heard him?

REBECCA HANNETT: Yeah. We heard a noise. We'd all heard about that shrimp boat and the guys who'd been eaten on it, and when we heard the noise in the shrubs it sort of made us all go quiet. We were scared, you know?

DETECTIVE TRAVIS: I know. Tell me what happened?

REBECCA HANNETT: Well, we didn't know what it was, you know, in the shrubs. We just...well, I heard it, and I went kind of numb, you know? Do you know that feeling? When all of the sudden you just go numb inside?

DETECTIVE TRAVIS: Yes, I know it. You're scared. Something's not right?

REBECCA HANNETT: Exactly. I heard that noise and I looked up from the lock and Jennifer and Heather were both looking toward the shrubs. And then he charged us. He came tearing out of the shrubs all growly and mean...and then he killed them.

DETECTIVE TRAVIS: He? You mean the hairy man you told me about earlier?

REBECCA HANNETT: Yes, the hairy man.

DETECTIVE TRAVIS: Tell me what he did.

REBECCA HANNETT: He came running across the lawn, but not really...not really...

DETECTIVE TRAVIS: Becca, what? Not really what?

REBECCA HANNETT: Not really running. It was like he was on all fours, you know? Kind of bounding across the lawn, like a dog or something.

DETECTIVE TRAVIS: He was running at you on all fours?

DETECTIVE TRAVIS: Becca, answer me with your words.

REBECCA HANNETT: Yes.

DETECTIVE TRAVIS: And what happened next?

REBECCA HANNETT: He killed Heather. He grabbed her by her hair and pulled her down to the ground and bit a big chunk out of her neck. She never even had a chance to cry out.

DETECTIVE TRAVIS: And Jennifer?

REBECCA HANNETT: He got on top of her and clawed at her face with his hands. I saw blood go all over the place.

DETECTIVE TRAVIS: And then?

REBECCA HANNETT: I ran.

DETECTIVE TRAVIS: What happened? Did he come after you?

DETECTIVE TRAVIS: Becca, I can see you nodding? Did he come after you?

REBECCA HANNETT: Yes.

DETECTIVE TRAVIS: But you got away.

DETECTIVE TRAVIS: Becca, how did you get away?

REBECCA HANNETT: I got as far as the other side of the street. He caught me and knocked me down and started tearing the clothes off my back.

DETECTIVE TRAVIS: What did you do, Becca?

REBECCA HANNETT: I put my hands over my head and prayed for it to stop.

DETECTIVE TRAVIS: And what happened then?

REBECCA HANNETT: It did.

DETECTIVE TRAVIS: He stopped?

REBECCA HANNETT: Yes. He leaned down and I felt his breath on my face. He smelled like something had died inside him, all rotten, you know? And then he sniffed me.

DETECTIVE TRAVIS: He sniffed you?

REBECCA HANNETT: He smelled me, like he was, I don't know, trying to mark my scent or something. I was scared.

DETECTIVE TRAVIS: But he stopped tearing at your clothes?

REBECCA HANNETT: I don't know. I guess. I just remember the shot. The guy who lives across the street from Heather came out in his bathrobe and he fired off a shot. The hairy man took off after that.

DETECTIVE TRAVIS: And what did you do?

DETECTIVE TRAVIS: Becca? What did you do then?

REBECCA HANNETT: I just dropped my face in the grass and cried.

* * *

I read through the police report several times over the next few days, and though I had a bunch of chances to tell the guys about it, I didn't. I don't know why. I guess I felt like I just didn't understand my feelings enough to talk about them. Like anything I said would just be a fumbling mess rather than get at the emptiness that was swelling inside me.

I'd never known anyone who died before, much less been murdered.

There was a kid named Armand Resendez in my 6th grade class who accidentally shot himself with his dad's gun, but I hadn't really known him, and his death was, forgive me, just a curiosity.

But Heather was more than that.

She meant something to me–a great deal, actually–and I ached inside, even when I wasn't thinking about her. I didn't say anything about this to the other guys because I couldn't quite wrap my mind around her being gone and I hated fumbling around with my words when I was trying to talk about something important. Once, I tried to say something to Jeff about it. I started to talk about how much it hurt. I said, "Alan's sister, you know, Heather…"

"Yeah, that sucked, didn't it? Alan, that poor guy. He's a mess about it. Dude, she was hot though, wasn't she?"

I said nothing.

I was appalled at what he'd said, at the way he'd trivialized her…even though, to be honest, I'd done the same thing that day I talked with her in her parents' kitchen.

Heather, reduced to *Dude, she was hot though, wasn't she?* seemed so vulgar, so cruel, so completely and utterly empty of understanding.

I wanted to cry.

I told him I had to take a piss and walked out of the room.

I was unable to catch my breath.

I wanted to hit something. I wanted to lash out with my fists and scream at the sky and tell God he was an obscene joke.

I was still feeling that vague and unfocused rage five days later, at Heather's funeral. I stood next to my mom and dad and listened to my mother weep. There were hundreds of people in the crowd. Lots and lots of kids from Clear Lake High School. Lots and lots of kids from Clear Lake Intermediate School, too. Kids I knew. All the girls wore black dresses. The boys wore suits that didn't seem to fit quite right. Everybody wore a look of uncertainty. We were all young, and death was a faraway and foreign land. Heather had been one of us, but we were still us. We were kids, and when you put us together, so many of us, it couldn't help but be a good time. Everybody forced themselves to hide this, but I saw it just the same in everybody's faces. The boys and the girls were like horses eager to break loose from the bridle. They wanted to run free together, to hang, because death was so far away, so unreal, so improbable. Yet their sense of decorum held them in place. They shifted on uneasy feet, some even wept, even though I doubt a one of them felt the confusion and fear and rage and inexplicable pain that ran through me. I looked around the crowd and I held back my tears and I hated them all, every single one of them.

Until I realized I was being self-righteous in my misery.

What right did I have to resent the others for their levity? They were teenagers on summer vacation, after all. Same as me. They all knew Heather, all felt her absence. Wasn't it possible they ached as much as I did? Wasn't it possible that, though they appeared to be more interested in each other than in the reason they'd all gathered here, that they still felt pain as sincere as mine?

And wasn't it incredibly self-obsessed to be thinking like this while Heather (he ripped the meat out of her throat with his teeth) lay in the silent ground?

I still found it hard to breathe.

I still felt stupid before the questions I knew needed answering.

Then I looked across the grave and saw Alan standing next to his mom and dad, and I knew instantly that I didn't understand grief, or dying, or the sense of utter and irrefutably profound loss the way that Alan did.

He looked empty.

Later, after the priest had read from the Bible and the family had put flowers in the grave, I tried to talk to Alan. I thought, maybe, I could talk to him.

But it was no good.

I said, "Hey, man, I'm so sorry…" He turned away without giving me a chance to finish. "Alan, wait…"

He didn't even look back. He went over to his mother's side and pressed himself against her and she put her arm over his shoulder. A veil seemed to fall over them, one that I couldn't penetrate. One that I wasn't worthy to enter. They were one in their unfathomable hurt.

I looked away, embarrassed at my clumsiness.

He needed more than I could offer, and I didn't even know where to begin.

* * *

Alan remained apart from us.

As the next few days rolled away, and became one week, and then two, he still refused to speak to us, to let us be a part of his life. When the phone service came back on, I tried calling him. He hung up on me. I went to go see him. He answered the door, then started to close it without a word. Not angrily so. He looked tired, mentally and physical exhausted. Beat down even.

I put a hand on the door and said, "Hey, Alan."

He just stared at me.

"Hey, it's me. It's Mark. Remember, your friend."

"I'm tired," he said.

"And I'm worried sick for you. What's going on? I want to help you, if you'll let me."

"You can't help, Mark. Listen, don't come around anymore, okay? Don't bother calling."

"Jesus, Alan, where's this coming from?"

He just gave me a sad shake of his head and closed the door.

Later that afternoon Eric and Jeff came over to spend the night and I told them about it. "He did the same to me," Eric said. "Poor guy is spiraling down the bowl."

"You don't think he'd…" I made a slash across my wrist with my finger. "You know, hurt himself?"

Jeff gave that some thought. "No, I don't think so. I think he's just taking it really hard. I mean, his sister…Jesus."

"Yeah," I said.

We were in the kitchen, drinking Sprites and making a huge mound of nachos. My parents were at a movie, one of the rare times they ever got to go out together, and they'd left the three of us to ourselves. My mom had taken me to the video store earlier that day and I'd picked up three of the best films from 1981: *An*

American Werewolf in London; *Wolfen*; and *The Howling*. It was going to be a late night.

"What does your dad think about it?" Eric asked.

When I didn't answer right away, Jeff looked up from the nachos. They were both looking at me now, waiting for an answer.

"You guys want to see something?" I said.

They looked at each other and shrugged. "Sure," Jeff said. "As long as it's not another gun."

"Ha," I said. "No, this is something else. Come on."

I took them to my dad's study.

Jeff clapped his hands and said, "Alright, more *Playboys*?"

"No," I said. "This is serious."

Jeff raised his eyebrows, but said nothing. I took out the *Playboy* and set it aside. The case file was still there. I checked it whenever I got the chance, because sometimes Detective Travis would feed my dad some new information, but nothing of substance had been added for nearly a week. The killings had stopped after the attack on Heather and Jennifer, and the lack of any real updates made me worried that maybe the trail had gone cold.

But Eric and Jeff didn't know about any of that. When I took the file out and handed it to Jeff, he stared at it like it was a winning lottery ticket.

"Is this what I think it is?"

I nodded.

"You've had this and you didn't show it to us?"

I shrugged. "I was gonna show it to you guys soon enough. It just felt, I don't know, too soon before."

"Can I…?" He held up the file.

"Sure," I said. "That's why I got it out."

We took the case file to the kitchen and sat at the table and Jeff and Eric took turns passing documents back and forth. Eric was looking at the pictures while Jeff was reading Becca Hannett's statement. I watched his eyes as he skimmed the page. He hardly blinked. I think he was holding his breath, too.

"I didn't know they were eaten," he said, after finishing it.

"Yeah," Eric said. "Look, here's a picture."

Eric showed it to him and for a second I thought Jeff might hurl right there on the table.

"Oh man," he said. "Oh man, that's too much."

But it didn't stop him from reading more. Later, Eric tried to hand me one of the crime scene reports and I shook my head. "I've read everything in there at least five times."

He nodded. "This is just so unbelievable. They have all this, but they don't have the first clue as to who's doing this."

"Pretty much," I said.

We put the file back together and put it and the *Playboy* back in my dad's desk. Then we got the movies and the nachos and our drinks and went upstairs to watch our movies. Max came along, hoping for some of the nachos, no doubt. We set ourselves up in the media room and started in on *An American Werewolf in London*.

But none of us were really paying attention to the movie. We'd all seen it half a dozen times before, and what we really wanted to talk about was the information in that case file.

They knew everything I did now, and it felt somehow liberating. I wondered why I'd waited so long to show it to them. Perhaps I needed to shoulder the knowledge alone out of some kind of penance. I guess I felt that carrying that awful knowledge alone in some way honored Heather's life. I don't know. Maybe that's true, or maybe it was total bull crap. Who knows? I just know that I felt a whole lot better once the genie was out of the bottle.

"I just don't get how it's possible that nobody knows who this guy is," Eric said. "I mean, they don't have a main suspect, do they?"

"Not that I know of," I answered. "It'd be in the file if they did."

"So how are they going to figure it out?"

I told them what my dad had told me, how they would look into suspicious person calls around the shrimp camp from where the boat had originated, how they hoped to get lucky with something there.

"And of course they didn't," Eric said.

"Nope."

"So where do they go from here?" Jeff asked.

"My dad said they'd look at the forensics. Try to figure it out that way."

"But according to this, that's leading nowhere," Jeff said.

"What do you want me to say? If it was easy, anyone could do it."

"Well, yeah, but–"

Jeff was interrupted by Max. He'd just jumped to his feet and a terrible, stuttering growl was coming from somewhere deep inside him. His whole body looked coiled, the hair on his back standing on end, ears pulled back flush with his scalp.

He was focused on the TV, where David Naughton was making his first change into the werewolf. Hairs were sprouting on his arms. His face was stretching into a muzzle. His hands were turning into claws. It was a brilliant piece of movie magic. Clearly it had Max convinced. He looked about a heartbeat away from tearing into the screen.

"Max!" I shouted.

He looked back at me and barked.

"Dude, what's up with your dog?" Jeff said.

Eric, however, said nothing. He was leaning forward, staring at the TV, completely engrossed.

"Eric, what's up, man?" I said.

Slowly, he looked my way. "Remember in Becca's statement, what she called that guy, the Hairy Man?"

He pointed at the TV.

I laughed. "You're saying they were attacked by a werewolf? Dude, that's like, I don't know, disrespectful or something."

"But you read how she described the way he moved, how he growled at her."

"He's a lunatic," I said, as though that explained it all. But I could see his mind working, and he had the look of a man who is witnessing all the pieces come together. I turned to Jeff. "Dude, help me out. People don't turn into wolves. That's just movie stuff."

But Jeff said nothing. He made a helpless sort of shrug.

"Really?" I said. "You too? Guys, come on. Whoever this guy is he's just a lunatic, not a werewolf."

"Do you have an almanac?" Eric said.

"I, well…yeah, I guess. Downstairs, probably. In my mom's office."

Eric ran for the stairs. Jeff and I traded a quick look, then followed along. Eric grabbed the almanac from my mom's bookshelf and flipped to the index.

"The hurricane was on June 24th, right?"

"Yeah," I said.

"And Mr. Moore was killed the day after that. And Heather the day after that?"

"Yes."

He suddenly punched the book with his finger and said, "Yes! That's it." He turned the book around so we could see it. It was open to a section showing the lunar calendar for the month of June. "See it?" he said. "Look at when the moon's full. June 24th through the 26th, 1983, the same days as the murders."

Beside me, Jeff whistled.

"So? That doesn't prove anything," I said. "And besides, a few days ago you were saying the Houston Police Department faked Dean Corll's death and that he was the one doing this."

"It's not Dean Corll," Eric said. "You read Becca Hannett's description of her attacker. The attacks happened during the full moon, and stopped right after. It seems pretty plain to me."

Jeff nodded. "Yeah, me too."

"Really?" I said. "A werewolf?"

I took the almanac from Eric and looked at the month of July. The next full moon was going to come July 19th, less than two weeks away.

If Eric and Jeff were right, and I wasn't even close to saying that they were, it was going to be a bloody summer.

* * *

Meanwhile, and this has nothing to do with the story I'm telling except to paint a picture of what the summer of 1983 was like for me, Jeff introduced me to the music of Pink Floyd. Like every other kid in America I'd heard "Another Brick in the Wall Part II" played on the radio and thought that it was catchy and cool and even a little subversive with its refrain of "We don't need no education..." But I'd not known, or rather, not appreciated, that the majesty that is Pink Floyd is only to be found deep in the album tracks. You have to get deep into Floyd for the music to come alive.

The same night we started talking about werewolves Jeff played *Dark Side of the Moon* for me.

I was hooked.

From the opening note, I was hooked.

We listened to it twice through and that second time around we turned out the lights and got on our backs and stared up at the ceiling lost up there in the darkness and let the music transport us to wherever our respective brains could take us. And when we got to the "Brain Damage/Eclipse" segue I swear I think I had an out-of-body experience. I really and truly felt like I was floating in the darkness, like it was pouring over me like water. It was terrifying and exhilarating at the same time. It pulled the breath from me. And I loved every moment of it.

When it was done Jeff told me you could play *Dark Side* as a soundtrack for *The Wizard of Oz*.

"No way," I said.

"Dude, I'm not lying. Jake totally showed it to me."

Jake was Jeff's older brother, a total stoner. He was a senior at Texas Tech and didn't really seem to have much interest, or patience for that matter, when it came to Jeff and his friends. The few times I'd met him he'd been as red eyed as a Cylon warrior. Even a straight-laced kid like me had noticed the reek of marijuana and the slow, slurred speech.

"Your brother was probably high," I said. "Why in the world would a rock band waste their time making a soundtrack to a movie that our grandparents watched."

"Dude, you have to see it. I mean you've probably seen that movie, right? Right? But when you see it put to the Pink Floyd soundtrack, it'll change your brain. I couldn't believe it either, but there was this scene–you know the one where Dorothy's walking on that fence and teeters and falls–you know that one?"

"I don't know. It's been a while."

"Well, she does. And if you time it right–that's the thing: you have to start the record right after the lion roars for the third time–while she's teetering on that fence, the band is playing 'balanced on the biggest wave, race toward an early grave.' And then you know what happens?"

I shook my head.

"She falls into the pig pen. It's beautiful. And there are tons of moments like that. Seriously, watch it and listen. You'll totally get it."

More Pink Floyd would come that summer. *Wish You Were Here* was my personal favorite album, though I loved *Animals* and *The Wall* almost as much.

But my growing love of psychedelic rock was tainted by what I saw happening to Jeff. I've heard that apples don't fall very far from their trees, and while I don't know anything about Jeff's father, Dr. Collin Hefke, except that my mom said he was a well-respected cardiologist who taught at U of H, I saw the hero worship Jeff had for his older brother. Personally, as an only child, I didn't get it. If my older brother walked around wreathed in smoke and smelling of a Black Sabbath concert I'd have turned my back on him long ago; but then, as I said, that wasn't my situation. I knew enough to be quiet about things of which I had no knowledge.

I did, however, feel confident enough to respond to him when I got up to go to the bathroom in the middle of the night and found the TV still on and Jeff at the bathroom sink rolling a joint.

When I opened the door I scared him so bad he nearly spilled the weed all over the toilet. But then he chuckled kind of nervously and held the half-rolled joint up for me to see. "You want some?" he asked.

"Dude, get that out of my house right now."

"Whoa," he said. "It's cool."

"Like hell it is. My dad has a police dog downstairs. Do you honestly believe that Max won't immediately light on us the second he sees us?"

Jeff, and this surprised me, looked like he'd never considered that.

"What do I do?" he asked, still holding the half-rolled joint.

"Flush it, and don't ever bring that shit in my house again."

Jeff flushed the joint and the empty baggie it came in.

"Is that all of it?"

"Yeah," he said.

"Dude, what's wrong with you? Why would you bring that into my house?"

He shrugged. "I'm sorry. I didn't think it'd be that big of a deal."

"Well it is. How long have you been doing that anyway?"

He shrugged again. "I don't know. A couple of months."

"Did you get that from Jake?"

"Dude, what are you, my mother?"

"Whatever," I said. "Here, I gotta piss. Wash your hands first before you go back to bed. You're gonna have weed smell on your skin."

He washed his hands and went back to bed. I watched him head back down the hall and I couldn't believe it. My best friend was turning into somebody I didn't know, and worse, didn't care to know.

* * *

June was nearly over, but it had brought the end of school, the most terrible flood I'd ever seen or heard about, the shrimp boat, the alligator and all that came with that, Heather's and Mr. Moore's deaths, Jeff's drug use, and of course the wolf man, of whom I still refused to believe.

I refused to give up on my summer vacation, though. We hadn't been back to the Swamp since the flood, and I was curious to see what had become of it. So, the next day, a Tuesday it was,

Jeff and Eric and I got our pellet guns and Max and went out to see what the Swamp looked like.

We carried our guns by the breach, like World War II Marines trekking through the jungles of Indonesia, and crossed the strip of manicured grass at the edge of our subdivision, slid through a gap in the fence that was supposed to keep us kids out, and entered the Swamp. Once, while traipsing through the Swamp, I had seen a giant black snake slithering across one of the trails. I am terrified of snakes and I had never been that close to one so big. Scared half to death I jumped the thing and ran to beat the devil. That experience always came to mind whenever I entered the Swamp, reminding me that I had to be on my toes whenever I was in here. Like the alligator we'd destroyed by the scum pond, there was real wildlife in here. Suburbia was behind us.

But there was something else too. I'd heard my dad say that the land upon which our subdivision was built on had once been a vast cotton farm, and just a few hundred yards in from the fence was what I guess had once been a cotton processing facility. It was little more than three large, interconnected metal silos, nearly every inch of which was covered with graffiti. They were moldering rust heaps towering over a field of wrecked machine parts and Coke cans and used condoms, but I was drawn to it nonetheless. For me, those rusting silos held me with an irresistible gravity. They lit my imagination on fire, for when I stared at them, I saw city skylines in ruin. I turned the field of trash into rivers of wrecked and abandoned cars. That lonely collection of silos never failed to send me to dark and apocalyptic places, and I loved it for that.

"Come on," Jeff said, waving me on.

"I'm coming, I'm coming."

He and Eric were already pretty far ahead and Max and I had to trot to catch up. The storm had done some damage to the Swamp, but it wasn't as bad as I thought it'd be. The bits of garbage that hung from the trees and the shrubs were about what I expected. So too were the broken tree limbs. The odd thing though was the knot of grass and vines matted to the tops of the trees. I had seen the same thing in the gutters of my house after the water drained away, but to see it here, in the tops of the trees, meant that the water would have had to reach all the way up there, and some of those trees were twenty-five-feet tall. It made me wonder how the deer and the rabbits and all the other critters that lived out here had made it through the storm.

Clearly they had, though, for Max saw a whitetail deer and took off after it, barking like a dummy.

"You're not worried he's going to get lost?" Eric said.

"No, he'll be fine. Watch." I turned toward Max. "Max, come!"

Instantly his barking stopped. A moment later, he was crashing through the scrub brush and bounding onto the hard-packed dirt of the trail.

"See?" I said. "He's good."

Rather than answer, Eric let out a sharp cry of pain and clapped a hand over his cheek.

"What happened?" I asked.

He took his hand away, and I saw both his hand and cheek were wet with blood. And there was a nasty looking wound on his cheek.

"What the hell?"

"I think I got shot," he said.

"What?" Jeff said.

I stepped closer to study the wound and when I did something stung me on my forehead, just above the hairline. I cried out just as Eric had done, but when I touched my wound I felt a hard piece of metal stuck in my hair.

I held it out. "It's a pellet."

"Somebody's shooting at us," Jeff said.

"Billy," I said, and a moment later Billy and Matt Drake and Lee Johnson erupted from the trees behind us and charged.

"Oh shit," Eric said. "Run!"

I didn't need prompting. I took off as fast as I could go. Jeff and Eric took off in opposite directions, but it was obvious right from the get-go that Billy and his friends weren't interested in them. They wanted me, and they were coming on fast.

Max had wanted to stand his ground. As soon as Billy and the others broke from the trees he started to growl. I looked back and didn't see him. Instead I saw Billy gaining ground on me, his arms and legs pumping and pure hate and meanness in his glare.

"You better run, pussy!" he yelled at my back. "I'm coming for you."

I ducked my head and ran harder. We had reached an empty spot in the Swamp where there were no trees or shrubs, just waist-high grass for the next hundred yards or so. Up ahead was a thicket of trees. I knew I had to reach those if I had any hope of getting away. There was a wide ditch inside that thicket. If I could make it down into there I could choose from three different trails that led out the other side, and two of those went deeper into the Swamp, where the shrubs got really thick. It'd be the perfect way to escape.

Except I had to get there first.

Billy was gaining on me still. I could hear his breathing. I could almost feel his hands on my back. I chanced a glance over my shoulder and saw he was right behind me. Matt and Lee looked like they were getting tired. They had fallen behind, and Lee was actually slowing to a walk and holding his side.

Not Billy though.

Billy was right on my back. He couldn't have been less than ten feet behind me when we reached the trees. I slammed into a screen of limbs and leaves and rolled to the left because I knew these woods well. The tree limbs gave way for me and I paused only long enough to bend the biggest of the branches back and let it go. It snapped back into place just as Billy got there and smacked him in the face.

He barked in surprise.

He thrashed at the branches, trying to get them out of his way.

I used the few seconds I'd bought to sprint to the side of the ditch and slide down the steep muddy bank to the tangled screen of weeds and shrubs below. I sank to my knees in water left over from the storm. But I wasn't about to let it slow me down. I ran for the opposite end of the ditch, where it opened onto the outgoing trails and offered a way out.

From above me I heard Matt Drake say, "Where'd he go?"

"He's down there," Billy said. "Move."

I turned and saw Billy and Matt standing at the edge of the ditch. Lee Johnson came up beside them a moment later, chest heaving like he was about to puke from the exertion of the sprint.

"How the hell are we supposed to get down there?" Matt said.

I took up my pellet gun and fired for Billy's face. I think I hit him in the cheek, but I'm not sure, because right after I pulled the trigger and saw him flinch, confirming the hit, I turned and ran. He screamed that he was going kill me, but at that point I knew I had the advantage. I was in known territory, home turf, and he couldn't touch me.

All I had to do was stay quiet.

I took the left fork when the trail opened into three possible choices. The middle way had a dense screen of limbs and leaves right at the head, and to get through it would have definitely left a mark and probably made a lot of noise. I didn't think Billy and his crew were smart enough to read the language of spoor, but they could certainly hear me busting through the underbrush.

The trail I was on was made of packed white dirt. My mud-soaked tennis shoes would leave footprints anybody with eyes could follow. Realizing this, I jumped into the grass that grew alongside the trail and took off running. That grass was perfect snake country, but at the moment my fear of what Billy would do to me far outweighed the nebulous fear that a snake might be lurking underfoot.

I ran like hell.

I ran until I reached another stand of oaks and hackberry and there I dropped to the ground and crawled under a tangle of leaves and branches that I hoped would hide me. My lungs were burning and I was too exhausted for another foot chase.

Then I heard Billy and Matt coming up the trail.

"You think he made it this far?" Matt said.

"I don't know. Maybe. Hey, look at that."

I couldn't see them, and I doubted they could see me. I listened to see if they were coming my way. If they were, I'd have to run again.

But they were going the opposite way. I could hear them crashing around in the tall weeds that grew next to the trail.

"What's that for?" Matt asked.

"What do you think? I'm going beat his ass with this."

A pause.

"I don't know," Matt said. "You could really hurt him with that."

"No shit, Sherlock. What do you think I'm trying to do here?"

"Yeah, but…that thing could do a lot of damage. I mean, like, put him in the hospital damage."

"That's the idea."

Oh crap, I thought. I was still breathing hard, trying to catch my breath, and no matter how hard I tried, my breathing sounded way too loud. "Please don't do this," I told myself. "Be quiet, be quiet."

"Yeah, but we gotta find him first," Matt said.

"Shhh," Billy said. "Be quiet for a second."

Ah crap, I thought, and held my breath. My lungs felt like they were going to catch fire they hurt so badly, but I held my breath.

"I want to go back and get Lee. There were three trails back there. We'll each walk one. We're pretty far out. He probably won't want to go much farther. It should only be a matter of time before we catch up with him. When we do, we'll bring him back to the fork and wait for the others to come back."

"Unless it's you that catches him."

"Yeah. If so I'm gonna leave his dead ass out here. I bet we could put him next to a pond. Shouldn't be long before an alligator finds him."

"Dude, that's hardcore."

"Can you think of any little shit who deserves it more?"

I listened to this with my lungs still burning. It sounded like they were headed away from me, back down the trail; but I knew Billy, and that was just the kind of trick he'd use. Get a little ways off and wait, the whole dialogue between he and Matt just a diversion to get me to give myself away.

But I couldn't hold my breath any longer.

I let it out and then took a deep breath.

I waited.

Still, the sound of them walking away.

I took a chance and parted the screen of leaves I was using for cover and saw them walking off, not bothering to look back.

So it wasn't a trick.

Good to know.

I slowly got to my feet, careful not to disturb the branches around me, and headed off down the trail. I walked through the copse of trees to the next clearing and I broke into a run. There was no way in hell Billy and his crazy ass friends were going to catch me out here alone.

I ran.

I ran like hell.

* * *

Finally, I had to stop.

Breathing hard, I turned and looked back over the path I'd taken. Billy and his friends were nowhere to be seen, and that was good, but I was further out than I'd ever been before, and that was not good.

Plus, I'd lost Max.

That was the really scary part.

Dad didn't mind that I took Max with me on my treks into the Swamp. His philosophy of dog handling was to fully integrate the dog into the home. He said he got a more energetic and better performing dog as a result. He said other K9 handlers believed in keeping the dog completely segregated from their families. But there was no one and only way to handle a police dog. Whatever worked was the right answer, he said. He said that if you got three handlers together and asked them about the right way to raise and train a police K9 the only thing you could be sure of two of them agreeing on was that the third guy was wrong.

There was one thing I could be sure of if I lost Max for good. My dad may not have kicked my ass for taking his gun out, but if I lost his dog, he surely would. Then he'd have to report it to the police department. Max was worth thousands of dollars, and represented three years of intensive training. My dad could lose his post as shift director for the HPD's K9 Unit. And he'd lose the respect of the cops under his command. It'd be proof positive that his way of caring for and training a dog was wrong.

And that wasn't even the worst of it. The worst of it was that I'd lose my best bud, my dog. I was already feeling like I was going to cry when I heard what sounded like a bark coming from somewhere ahead of me.

I listened, but didn't call out. I couldn't take that chance, not with Billy and his friends possibly close by.

I walked out of the copse of trees in which I stopped to rest and saw an old rundown house. It was completely abandoned, and had been for years. There was no glass in the windows, and the front door was missing. The roof had holes in it and sagged down at one corner like the brim of an old floppy hat. Yellow shoots of Johnson grass grew up all around it, making the house look like it had sunk down to its waist in the weeds. There was no yard to speak of, just patches of grass struggling to spread through bare earth.

The house was a surprise.

So too was the smell.

The stench of dead things hung in the air, heavy and cloying.

But the real shocker was the vast profusion of animal bones spread around the yard. I saw remnants of rabbits and birds and dogs and wild hogs and even the mangled carcass of a deer. Some of the skeletons appeared to have been stripped completely of the flesh and had bleached white in the sun. Others still had blackened bits of rotten meat clumped on them. The deer, mangled as it was, almost looked fresh, maybe a day or two old.

I wandered around the yard, studying the house. Flies buzzed around my face and I swatted them away. Small bones crunched beneath my feet. I wondered what this place was. I figured it was the home of whoever owned the cotton farm of which all this land was a part, which meant that it had to have been abandoned at least thirty years earlier. But it was the bones that really made me wonder. Was this some kind of animal dying place, like those famed elephant graveyards I was always reading about in my H. Rider Haggard novels, or was it the feeding ground for a predator, like a cougar or a pack of coyotes? The coyotes seemed like the best bet, and if it was a bunch of coyotes that would also explain the barking.

That was what I was thinking anyway, when I heard bones crunching behind me.

With a skipped heartbeat I wheeled around and saw a naked man crouching at the far corner of the yard, staring at me, not blinking, and not sane.

He was the hairiest man I'd ever seen. He had a ragged beard with all sorts of unidentifiable things tangled in it, and long scraggly hair and thick black hair on his arms and chest and legs.

But it was his eyes that held me.

He stared at me, and when his gaze narrowed, I felt like I'd just been put in the crosshairs of a hate so singular and violent it was like I owed him money.

I paled from that. I fell back.

He growled. It was a doglike sound, guttural, from the back of his throat, and it caused me to take another few steps back.

Then he charged.

He ran in a crouch, arms swinging in an almost apelike fashion, his knuckles grazing the grass, but all the while snarling, his eyes locked on me.

I was so startled it took me a moment to react, but when I did I screamed and turned and ran as fast as I could.

He was right behind me, his snarls turning into something that was very close to words but inarticulate for the fury behind them.

I veered left, toward the house. I jumped onto the porch where the front steps were missing, narrowly dodged a rotted hole in the wooden floor, and entered the house. There was trash all over the floor, mildewing furniture pressed up against the wall, picture frames crashed in piles near the angle where the floors met the walls. I saw it all in a blur as I sprinted through one room after another, that snarling, raging, lunatic man at my heels.

Then I turned a corner and found myself rushing headlong toward the back porch. There was a rotten hole in the wooden floor and I jumped it. I landed on soft wood that snapped beneath my feet, but barely held. I jumped again from the porch to the bare dirt of the yard and kept on running.

Behind me, the hairy man's snarls suddenly turned to a whimper of pain.

It was unmistakable. A yap, followed by a whining groan.

I turned and saw him half buried in the wooden porch that had snapped, but held, beneath my weight.

It hadn't held for him. His right leg was buried to the thigh in broken wooden timbers and he was trying to jerk himself loose at the cost of tremendous pain.

I didn't waste the opportunity.

I ran for the trail.

Screw Billy and his gang. Let them catch me now. Let the hairy man come on too. Maybe they'd attack each other and end all my problems, even though I knew, even as I ran, that probably wouldn't happen.

I looked back to see the hairy man pulling himself out of the hole in the floor. His leg was all bloody from midthigh down past his knee, but it didn't look like it was going to slow him down any. He sighted in on me again and ran after me. With a scream I redoubled my pace, and by the time I'd reached the tall grass, with only twenty yards to go to reach the cover of the trees–or what I hoped would be cover, as it had been when I was running from Billy–my lungs were burning. My heart was hammering against my chest so hard I felt like it was going to burst. But I could hear the hairy man gaining on me. I could hear the awful slathering sound his breathing made, punctuated by grunts and a sharp, piercing growl. He was right behind me, and I didn't dare look back. All I had to do was reach the cover of–

He hit me hard on the back of my shoulders, knocking me to the ground.

I fell over forward and rolled into the tall grass next to the trail.

With a whimper I tried to scurry back to my feet, but it did no good. He was all over me. He pounded on my head and tore into the skin on my arms with nails that felt sharp as a frayed piece of metal.

I didn't realize at first he was trying to flip me over onto my back. It felt like he was trying to dig a hole through my back down to my heart. But then he managed to get a grip on my elbow and pulled me roughly up and twisted me around so that I landed on my back. The impact knocked the breath from my lungs and for a moment I couldn't breathe.

I was staring at him then. I smelled the fetid odor of rot on his breath. I looked into his bloodshot eyes. I saw the mud and twigs matted into the hair of his beard and saw bugs crawling in his hair. Then he growled at me, showing his teeth, and they were blackened with clotted blood.

"Please, don't," I managed to choke out.

His lips remained curled away from his teeth. Hate, a venomous, savage hate, lit his gaze.

He knelt closer and sniffed me.

I couldn't breathe. I just waited, pinned there beneath his weight, trembling from head to foot. The one thought flooding out all else in my mind was that I didn't want to die. Please don't let me die.

Something flashed out of the corner of my eye.

The hairy man's lips uncurled and he looked up just as Max crashed into him from the side. Dog and hairy man went tumbling into the tall grass. It took me a moment to realize what was going on, but when I did I quickly jumped to my feet and ran a few steps toward the trees.

I stopped when I heard Max. Looking back I saw a dog I didn't recognize. It was Max all right, but he was in berserker mode. His fur was standing all on end. Ferociously loud stuttering growls seemed to come from deep inside him. He was relentless in his attack. I'd been threatened by some of the dogs in my neighborhood before. They'd seemed mean enough, yet they were slow to charge, as though trying to break my confidence with their threats and make me run. Not Max. He was all teeth and volume, tearing into the hairy man with a violence that shocked me. It was hard to believe this was the same dog whose enormous chest I had used for a pillow while watching horror movies. It was hard to believe he was the same dog that, when Lisa Rodriguez and I were on the couch together, sitting close, had climbed up and sandwiched his butt down between us, leaning against me and giving her a jealous sneer. If that was the dog that fought side by side with my dad up in Houston's 2nd Ward, then I felt sorry for the bad guys.

But then the hairy man grabbed Max in a bear hug and threw him into the grass. I saw the hairy man raise his face to the sky, open his bloodstained mouth, and bite down on my dog.

Max's growls turned to a pained whimper, and when he rolled out from under the hairy man and got to his feet, his right ear was covered in blood.

Somehow, Max broke loose from him and ran back to the trail. Hurt as he was, he still managed to put himself between the hairy man and me. The hairy man charged us in that weird, loping, apelike run of his, but he had barely covered a few steps before Max charged him again.

The hairy man got a face full of fangs and fell back.

Max disengaged too.

He backed up, his eyes still lasered in on the hairy man.

I turned and ran toward the trees, and when I looked back I saw Max coming up behind me and, off in the distance, the hairy man, watching us.

Max and I ducked into the trees and ran for home.

From behind us, I could hear the hairy man howling in rage.

But he didn't follow.

* * *

On the way home I stopped by a house that looked like nobody was home and used the garden hose to clean Max's injured ear. He flinched away from the cold water with a whimper, but finally let me clean him off. The wound didn't look as bad as I thought it would. There was a lot of blood, but after I washed it off and used my shirt to staunch the wound, it started to look a lot better, but I knew there was still a risk of infection. I had to get him home and let my mom look at him.

First I had a debt of gratitude to acknowledge. I took his head in my hands and put my forehead on the top of his muzzle. "You saved my life back there, Max," I said.

He licked my face until I started to laugh and finally pushed him away. Not very hard, though.

"You're a good dog, Max. I love you. You ready to go home?"

He barked once.

I patted his flank and we walked the greenbelt back home. It was probably not the smartest way home, considering Billy and his gang were still looking for me, but at that point I just didn't care. I was too exhausted. And, believe it or not, the farther I got from the Swamp, the more unreal what I'd just encountered seemed, like it was a bad dream or something. The fear I'd felt out in the wild country had subsided, leaving me numb, and that's how I was feeling when Max and I walked in the back door.

I started to call out, but before I could I heard my mom and dad arguing from my mom's study.

"I don't want to argue about this anymore," Dad said. "I'm tired."

"I'm not arguing. And I'm tired too, Wes. I'm just so tired of this schedule. We never see each other. Either I'm working or you're working. It's hard. That's all I'm saying. I'm not trying to blame you."

"Blame me? Oh Jesus Christ, Meredith. What the hell do you expect me to do about it?"

"Please don't yell."

"I'm not yelling. Jesus, I don't get where this is fucking coming from. I mean, what the hell?"

My mom didn't answer.

"Well? Christ, I've been working this schedule for eight years. Why are you all bent out of shape now?"

I thought I heard her crying.

"Oh Christ, really? I'm not gonna deal with you if you're crying."

He came around the corner from the entryway then and saw me. He stopped in his tracks. "Holy hell, what'd you do to my dog?"

Dad took a few steps forward before he noticed me. From my hair down to my shoes I was one big grass and dirt stain. And there was blood on my shirt. Some of it mine, some of it Max's.

"Mark, what happened?"

He came forward and took my shoulders in his hands. Mom came around the corner behind him, drying her eyes with the back of her hand.

Then she saw me and she turned all business.

She pushed her way around my dad and took my face in her hands. She looked into my eyes, then checked my ears, my neck, my arms and hands.

"What happened to you?" she asked. "Something happened?"

"I saw him," I said.

"Who?" my dad asked. "Did somebody try to hurt you?"

I nodded. "Max fought him off me. He bit Max's ear. Nearly tore it off."

"Who?" he insisted. "Do you know who did this to you?"

I nodded again.

"Who, damn it?"

I swallowed. It was hard to get it down. "The hairy man," I said.

"Who?" my mom asked.

I looked at my dad, and I could tell from the ashen color that had descended over his features that he understood exactly who I meant.

* * *

I told them everything.

Then I told the detectives from the Harris County Sheriff's Office the same thing a bunch more times.

They showed me photos, a bunch of photos, and asked me over and over again if I was sure this wasn't the guy.

No?

Well, what about this one?

Or this one?

I shook my head to all of them.

Finally, I guess, they'd figured I'd had enough and passed me off to my mother, who sat with me on a long wooden bench, like a pew, in the hall outside the Homicide Office. Through a few panes of glass I could see my dad inside, arguing with Detective Travis. I wanted to know what they were arguing about, but I couldn't hear them, and I couldn't read their lips. All I could tell was that they were pissed at each other.

Later, my mom drove me home.

"Your dad and I talked it over," she said when we were in the kitchen. "I don't want you to go out and about by yourself."

"Mom," I said, "I wasn't…I wasn't alone. Jeff and Eric were with me. And I had Max."

"I mean…without one of us."

"You mean, you and Dad?"

"Yes."

"Uh," I said, and had no idea how to continue. "Mom, it's…it's summer."

She drew a deep breath and let it out. She looked suddenly tired and worried and sad all at the same time. "I'm sorry," she said. "I know it's your summer vacation. I'm sorry."

"But Mom…"

She turned away. She opened the fridge and pulled out a half-full bottle of white wine and poured herself the tallest glass I'd ever seen her pour. Mom took a sip and set the glass down next to the sink.

"Go upstairs," she said.

"But Mom…"

"You don't have to go to bed. Just go upstairs. Watch TV, read, I don't care." Her voice had been steadily rising until she was almost yelling at me, but she suddenly broke off with that last little bit about not caring. When she spoke again, she sounded put upon and worn down. "Just go upstairs."

I didn't bother to argue. Had it been my father delivering the same set of marching orders, my pride probably would have insisted on a fight. At the very least some heated shouting on both sides. With my mother there was none of that. She possessed a sort of witching absolutism that broached no retort. I didn't dare respond.

Instead, I slinked off up the stairs, turned on the TV, and found nothing I wanted to watch, so I turned that off and went to the bookshelf. There I found a tattered copy of *Dr. Jekyll and Mr. Hyde* and resigned myself to spend an evening with Robert Louis Stevenson.

I read it in the chair I kept next to my window.

Some few minutes later, I put the open book down on my lap and pressed my face against the glass, for I had heard a noise.

The guttural chopping noise of a helicopter flying overhead, bearing north.

I watched it sprint overhead, and though I didn't know it for sure I sensed it in my gut that this was the vanguard of the police manhunt for the hairy man Max and I had battled that very afternoon.

Somewhere out there, my dad and Max were no doubt gearing up to storm the little abandoned farmhouse where I'd nearly lost my life just a few hours earlier.

The hairy man, if he was still there, was about to meet the police.

He was about to meet my dad.

* * *

I waited up all that night in the hopes that my dad would come home and let me know what happened.

That didn't happen.

I read until my eyes got tired then turned on cable and found a lot of nothing to watch. Around three in the morning I got hungry and went downstairs. I stepped carefully through the living room, not wanting to wake my mom, but in the silence of our darkened house I heard her sobbing in her room. I went over to her door and looked through the crack to where she lay stretched out on her bed, her back to me. Her shoulders were hitching with each sob and every once in a while she'd sniffle.

I wanted to say something, but I felt like I'd only make a muddled mess of it. I was never any good at that sort of thing. I'd been useless to say anything meaningful to Alan when he needed a friend, and he'd ended up pushing me away. I looked in on my mom and I was terrified I'd repeat the same mistake with her.

So I turned away from the door and went into the kitchen. My mom had gone shopping since the storm, but the fridge was still relatively empty. I found some peanut butter, some honey, a little raspberry jelly, and I mixed it all together in a bowl of yoghurt and dropped down at the kitchen table to eat.

I had the spoon nearly to my lips when I saw a flash of white in the living room.

I looked up, expecting to see my mom in her nightgown, and instead caught a glimpse of Heather Crawford in a white dress. She was covered head to toe in blood.

With a skipped heartbeat I dropped the spoon to my bowl and stood up, the chair skidding across the tiled floor.

"Heather?" I said.

But she was gone.

In the time it took me to get to my feet and call out to her, she was gone.

I shook my head. I blinked at the empty darkness where I could have sworn she stood just a moment before. Confused and frightened, I tried to swallow the lump in my throat but couldn't quite do it.

Dimly, I became aware of the tremor in my breathing. My skin felt hot, my fingers numb. I needed to sit down and catch my breath. I dropped heavily into the kitchen chair, still staring at the empty living room. To be honest, I was afraid to look away, for I realized then that I had seen a ghost. Even if for just a moment, I had seen a ghost. I had never thought I'd be the kind to believe in ghosts. I thought I was more of a materialist than that.

But my fear taught me the truth.

I believed in ghosts.

* * *

My dad woke me up the next morning. He was covered in sweat and mud, and there was a look of frustrated exhaustion on his face.

"We found the house, just like you said."

"And the hairy man?" I asked.

Dad shook his head.

"He was there, Dad. I swear it."

"I know. We found blood in that hole near the back porch where he fell through. We found a lot of chewed on bones too. Some of the CSI guys told me they might be able to match bite marks to the marks on Heather and her friend."

"But you didn't find him?"

"No, I'm afraid not, Mark."

"So…what's the next move?"

He looked down at his hands. His knuckles were caked with dirt. "Listen, Mark, I don't want you to go out for a while."

"You mean, to the Swamp?"

"No, I mean out. At all. I don't want you running around without your mom or me with you."

"I don't understand. You're grounding me?"

"No, Mark. No, that's not it. Mark, this scares me, and I don't like being scared. I looked around that place. I saw the bite mark on Max's ear. It scared me, Mark. I don't want to lose you. You understand, don't you?"

I didn't know what to say. Finally, I answered him with a shrug.

"I love you, Mark. You'll do as I say, won't you? You'll stay indoors until I can get this guy."

I could have argued, but I didn't.

Instead I lowered my head and nodded.

"Good boy," he said. He went to the door of my bedroom, turned, and said, "I love you, Mark. You know that, right?"

"Yeah," I said. "I love you too, Dad."

He nodded, and closed my door behind him as he left.

* * *

That afternoon, right after my dad and Max had left for work and my mom was still at her practice, I went around the house and gathered together every book I could find that might have something in it on werewolves. Knowledge is power, as they say, and I was determined to learn all I could. The thing about it was that up until then I'd been sure that Jeff and Eric were being ridiculous with all their talk of werewolves, but after seeing the hairy man in person I was a lot less sure of myself. The hairy man's eyes had been those of a feral animal, not a sane man's. All that hair, and the way he'd attacked me and fought with Max; it just seemed like too many coincidences piled on top of each other. Maybe there was something to the whole werewolf thing after all.

I read my mom's books until she came home, around 7 o'clock that evening. I went through Ovid's *Metamorphoses,* Pliny the Elder's *Natural History,* Sir Thomas Browne's *Pseudodoxia Epidemica,* Grimm's *Fairy Tales,* and even the *Encyclopedia Britannica,* and in the end came up with a whole lot of nothing. I found a lot on werewolves, but none of it matched anything else and all of it was different from the accepted conventions of the Hollywood wolf man.

In some accounts the werewolf transformed into an actual wolf, only larger and without a tail. In others, he retained his human mind, while in others he was carried away by pure animal lusts. Some authors said that you became a werewolf by putting on magical girdles or belts. Some said that you became a werewolf by applying a salve. Still others claimed the change was brought about by a deal with the devil, or through witchcraft. There was no mention of the wolfsbane used in the Lon Chaney Jr. films. Nor did the full moon seem to hold much importance. I was beginning to think none of these writers knew anything about their subject.

I got so into my reading that I didn't hear my mom come in.

"Mark?"

I looked up from the stack of books spread out on my bed. "Oh, hey Mom."

She was standing in the doorway, still holding her attaché case. "What are you reading? Is that my copy of Ovid?"

"Uh, yeah," I admitted.

She crossed the room to the side of my bed and picked up one of the books I'd stacked there. "Why are you reading Galen?" She picked up another book. "And Herodotus?" And another. "Sir Thomas Browne. Mark, what in the world is this?"

I didn't have an answer for her. The best I could do was shrug. Then she saw the *Encyclopedia Britannica* open to the entry on werewolves and the notes I'd made on one of her yellow legal pads and she put it together in about two seconds.

"Ah Mark, what are you doing?"

"Nothing," I said lamely.

She sat down on the side of my bed and looked at me with the sad, yet strangely sympathetic expression she reserved for times she felt like I really needed a long talking to about how the world worked. It was the same expression she'd worn when I admitted I was too vain to get braces, or when she'd come upstairs to find my bedroom door closed and me with my hand up Lisa Rodriguez's shirt. I hated that look.

"Your run-in with that man yesterday really scared you, didn't it?"

Of course it did, I thought.

But of course she already knew that.

That was how she worked these conversations. She'd start with a series of questions like that, obvious stuff, softening me up by forcing me to agree with her over and over until, when I finally disagreed, it threw me off balance. It was aggravating, but effective.

"I have to tell you it scared me," she said. "Detective Travis said he's pretty sure it's the same man who attacked Heather and her friends."

I watched my mom's eyes for some sign that she'd break down at the mention of Heather's name, but she seemed to be holding it together.

"You were lucky Max found you."

Again I nodded.

"Was that man really completely naked?"

"Yes."

"You said he was hairy. That's the same thing Rebecca Hannett said."

I shrugged. "Yeah, I guess."

She went over to my bookshelf and pulled down another volume of the encyclopedia. She flipped through some pages until she found the entry she was looking for, turned the volume around, and pointed at a picture. "Did he look like that?"

The picture showed a kid, about my age, sitting on some sort of fur-covered couch, holding a rifle and wearing what looked like a circus performer's outfit from the late 1800s. The caption said his name was Jo Jo, the dog-faced boy, a.k.a. Fedor Jeftichew.

"What is hypertrichosis?" I asked.

"A generic medical term for too much body hair. Is that what your hairy man looked like?"

I wanted to agree with her, but I couldn't.

"Not really," I said. "He didn't have *that* much hair. He had this long, scraggly beard and long, scraggly hair that looked like wires sticking up everywhere. All of it was kind of strawberry blond. You know that color, kind of red, kind of blond?"

She nodded.

"And his body was covered with hair too, but not like this. It didn't look like a circus freak show or anything. He was just, I don't know, hairy."

"Don't say freak show, Mark, please. I don't like that."

"Sorry."

"It's alright. I just don't like to hear you be mean. People like this can't help it."

I nodded. But she had me wondering. "Why'd you show this to me, Mom?"

"Well, first off, you know there's no such thing as werewolves, right?"

I didn't want to sound stupid by saying what I really thought, so I sort of shrugged.

"Right?" she said again.

"Well..."

"Oh Mark, no. Baby, listen to me. Werewolves are a fiction. They're nothing but folklore and the boogeymen of religious lunatics. Organizing the belief in God into religions is the sickest, vilest, most horrific and obscene act humanity has ever committed against itself. And a belief in werewolves is straight out of that superstitious nonsense. They're fine in horror movies, but to believe in them in real life is an insult to your native intelligence."

"But Mom, I..."

She said nothing. Just sat there looking at me, waiting for me to finish my thought.

"There's proof, Mom," I finally said, and there was as much defiance in my tone as I could muster.

"I'm listening."

"Well, he's called the hairy man for one."

"And...?"

"And the last time he killed people it was on the full moon. Look it up if you don't believe me. Jeff and Eric and I did. He murdered people three nights in row, and each night was a full moon. He hasn't killed anybody since then. Here, look." I slid off my bed and got the calendar from my desk. "See? I circled the dates from June. See the full moon symbol there in the corner?"

"Yes, I see it."

"That doesn't seem like strong evidence to you?"

"That this man is a werewolf?"

I paused. "Well, yeah," I finally said. It had been proof enough for me when Eric pointed it out to me. It had been proof enough to color my opinion with doubt anyway. But from the look on my mom's face, it clearly didn't mean anything to her.

"Mark," she said, "can I tell you something?"

"Sure," I answered, and dropped down into my desk chair.

"Some people say that the Catholic Church murdered more than fifty thousand people during the course of the Inquisition and the witch trials that went along with it. In a little over two hundred years, they systematically wiped out *fifty thousand* innocent lives. We're talking mostly women here, and nearly all of them poor and uneducated women from the fringes of European society. People like gypsies and Jews and newly converted pagans. We've led ourselves to believe this romanticized view of the witch trials that it was equals against equals, but that simply doesn't mesh with the facts. Real life isn't an Arthur Miller play. Nearly all of the Church's victims were poor farmers and herbalists and midwives whose only crime was not conforming to the mainstream. The Church picked off the low-hanging fruit in order to assert their dominance over the masses. Does this make sense to you, Mark? The Inquisition was never about good and evil, but about the Church asserting its political strength in Europe's yet to be assimilated frontiers. Do you understand?"

I wanted to say, No, Mom, I have absolutely no fucking idea what you're talking about, because I didn't. But instead I said, "Yeah, I guess."

"No, you don't. I can see that. I'm not being plain. I'm sorry. Look, superstition pisses me off. I'm sorry. Let me try to explain. During the height of the Inquisition, if you were odd, or crazy, you were going to be stigmatized. The Catholic Church was the biggest bully on the playground back then, and the weird kids, the helpless ones, those were the ones the Church picked on. Werewolves weren't a major part of the witch trials, but they did kill people for foolish beliefs like that, and they got their knowledge of what a werewolf was from the same books you're going over now. I'm begging you, don't re-create a dark and ignorant time. Don't look to superstition when the real truth is out there, just waiting for you to discover it."

I sat there sullenly. She was talking to me like an adult, and I appreciated that, but she could still make me feel a child when she gave me lectures and injunctions. Don't be ignorant. Don't be a superstitious fool. Let me tell you about the finer points of Medieval Church politics. I wanted to tell her that none of that meant a rat's ass to me, but I held my tongue because I knew I couldn't argue with her without sounding shrill and irrational, which would only prove her point and garner more lectures, more injunctions.

Instead I waited for her to speak.

Finally, she said, "Do you want to know what I think?"

"Sure," I said, but I'm afraid I sounded a little more petulant than I wanted to sound.

"I showed you that picture of Fedor Jeftichew because I wanted you to see how irrational people can be in the face of people strange to them. In the Middle Ages, and even later in some parts of Europe, he'd have been strung up as a werewolf for sure. And all for a random curveball in his genetic makeup. Luckily, there have been fewer than a hundred documented cases of extreme hypertrichosis since then. I say luckily, but really I shouldn't even say that. At least hypertrichosis was a strange enough sort of thing to make the uneducated and the ignorant local leaders of the day react along superstitious folk tale lines. But were they the real culprits of the day? No, I don't think so. I think the real culprit was the Church upper echelon trying to crush what it couldn't assimilate or understand. The confessions they obtained, whether under torture or at the threat of torture, were as fictitious as the werewolf itself. Your hairy man out there on the marsh, I think he's nothing but an insane homeless man who's seen too many bad movies. He's one of the ones the Church would have strung up for sure. He is the lurker on the threshold, the intruder, the Grendel, but he's no more a real monster of folklore than Richard Nixon or Pol Pot or Jim Jones."

"So, you don't think he deserves to be punished for what he did to Heather?" I asked.

She shook her head vigorously. "Absolutely not. I'm not one of those people who believe the criminally insane deserve a free pass just because they're insane. For what he did to you, and to Heather, I'd string him up myself. It's the calling him a werewolf that gets me mad, Mark. Do you see that? I believe you should call a thing what it is, and a crazy mass murderer is just that. Your hairy man is no more a werewolf than Jim Jones was a prophet."

She waited for a moment for me to say something, anything, but when I didn't she sighed and rose from the bed and went to my door.

"Mark, I want to smooth out all the wrinkles for you. I do. I want to blast away every roadblock you're ever gonna face. But I know I can't always do that. You're like your dad in so many ways...so strong, so brash. You've even got his good looks. But I think you got your hardheadedness from me. You've always had to find things out for yourself before you believe them. It was the same with me. Drove my dad crazy, and my mom even crazier. So if you need to find the answers out on your own, look up Johann Weyer. Read what he did, and then come down to dinner. I'm making a salmon loaf."

With that, she went downstairs.

It took me a while to look away from the empty doorway.

That was, without a doubt, the strangest, and yet the most honest, conversation I'd ever had with my mom, and I'd barely said three sentences to her during the whole of it.

But I knew enough to know that my mom was an intellectual force to be reckoned with. She was smart. And though I did a lot of dumb things as a teenager, ignoring her was not one of them. She was, after all, like a footnote that could not help but be followed once engaged.

I picked the W volume of the encyclopedia up from my bed and turned from *werewolf* to *Weyer, Johann (1515-1588)*, and started reading about the first real learned opponent of the Inquisition.

* * *

Dad, of course, wasn't home. During July and August my dad picked up lots of overtime from the swing shift guys. During those months my mom tended to move around the house like a woman half awake. When I finally made it downstairs there was a glass of Sprite over ice at my place at the table. My mom came from the kitchen carrying a glass of white wine for herself and a plate of salmon loaf and steamed broccoli for me. She sat at her place at the table and didn't eat. Just sat there sipping her wine.

"I read up on that Weyer guy," I said.

She took a long sip from her glass and made a noncommittal sound of encouragement.

"He was pretty brave to go against the Church like that, all those things he said about witches really being women suffering from a mental condition. Seems to me he was pretty far ahead of his time, sort of like a Sir Isaac Newton or a Charles Darwin nobody else has ever heard of. I can see why you admire him."

Another sip.

Only then did she seem to remember herself and put the glass down.

She straightened her napkin in her lap and smiled at me. "Yes, he was a very brave man, a real pioneer in mental health."

"The encyclopedia said he said witches suffered from melancholy. I thought that meant being sad."

"It meant all kinds of things back then," she said languidly, and took a long drink of her wine, nearly draining it.

"I heard the phone ring earlier," I said. "Was that Dad?"

She nodded. She looked unhappy, like she'd just tasted something bitter.

"Is everything all right?"

She stood up suddenly and went into the kitchen, standing at the sink with her back to me. I heard her sniffling as she poured herself another glass of wine.

"Mom?"

"I'm fine," she said. "Your dad's going to be working a double tonight. He'll be home tomorrow morning."

"Oh," I said.

"Eat your dinner, okay? I'll be back in a second. I'm gonna take off my makeup."

And just like that she was gone again. I took a long time to finish my dinner, hoping she'd come out of her room again, but she didn't. I washed off my plate and went upstairs to read *The Island of Dr. Moreau*.

* * *

Seeing as I wasn't allowed to go anywhere, my mom agreed to let Eric and Jeff spend the night. I guess she figured giving me a reason to stay in was better than giving me an excuse to sneak out. She even went to the video store for us and stocked the pantry with Cheetos and Sprites and Jiffy Pop. Our movies that night included *Alien*, *Invasion of the Body Snatchers*, and *Cat People*, which we all knew was a terrible film except that Nastassja Kinski was naked through most of it. We made popcorn, put some Sprites into a bucket of ice, and went upstairs to the media room.

Despite all my mom's preparations and good intentions, it was an awkward evening. None of us said much, at least at first. In fact, we were at the close of *Invasion of the Body Snatchers*, the part where Donald Sutherland points at the camera and makes that horrible open-mouthed moaning scream, before we came around to the thing we were all thinking about.

It was Eric who finally spilled it. "Tomorrow's the full moon," he said.

We traded glances. On the TV, the closing credits rolled.

Finally, Jeff nodded.

Then I nodded too.

"Do you think it'll start up again?" Eric said.

Jeff looked at me and frowned. I think all three of us were thinking of how long it had been since we'd seen Alan, and why.

"I think it will," Jeff said.

"Me too," I said.

Eric hung his head.

"We ought to think about protecting ourselves," Jeff said. "I mean, he came after you, Mark. If you hadn't had Max there, he'd have torn you to pieces."

"It wasn't even the full moon," Eric said. "Hell, it was broad daylight."

"Yeah, but I don't think that matters," Jeff said. "I mean, it matters, but, you know, not as much. The wolf man can still kill, even if it isn't a full moon."

"He wasn't a wolf man," I said. "He looked human enough to me."

"Well, of course," Jeff said. "I bet he only changes when it's the full moon. That's why I say we need to protect ourselves."

"How would we do that?" Eric asked.

"We've all got guns. Shotguns, I mean."

"But don't we need like silver bullets or something for that to work?" Eric said. "I don't have anything like that."

"I don't think so," Jeff said. "In *An American Werewolf in London* the villagers at the beginning of the movie shot the werewolf with regular shotguns."

"You don't know that," Eric said. "They could have used silver in their shot."

"Well, what about at the end of the movie? The cops shot the main character with rifles, and that killed him. I'm pretty sure the London Metropolitan Police Department doesn't issue silver-jacketed bullets. What do you think, Mark? The Houston Police Department wouldn't do that, would they?"

"Of course not."

Jeff turned to Eric and held up his hands as if that closed the matter. "See?"

"I just don't think we should take the chance, you know? If he comes into my house, I want to be prepared."

"You've got that .410 Browning your dad got you for Christmas last year. How much more prepared do you need to be?"

"I don't know," Eric answered. He looked miserable. "Do you think maybe the gun shops would have anything? I've seen those dragon breath shells they sell. You know the ones that make all that fire? Maybe they've got silver shot as well."

"I seriously doubt it," Jeff said. "Besides, it'd be ridiculously expensive."

"I've got some money saved up."

Jeff shrugged.

It was too much for me. I said, "Hey you guys, I've been thinking a lot about this. What if…what if this guy is just a guy, you know? Not a werewolf, but just some crazy homeless guy that likes to kill people."

"What do you mean?" Jeff asked.

"You know, maybe he just thinks he's a werewolf."

"No way," Jeff said. "A man couldn't tear people apart the way those bodies on the shrimp boat were torn apart."

"People can do all sorts of things if they believe they can," I countered.

"Why would anybody just think they're a werewolf?" Jeff said. "That's crazy."

"Which is exactly my point," I said. "Hell, back in the Middle Ages, the Church got people to confess to be witches and werewolves and all kinds of things."

"Yeah, by torturing them," Jeff said. "Plus, dude, this isn't the Middle Ages. Put in *Cat People,* would you? I want to see Nastassja Kinski naked." Then he turned to Eric and said, "Hey, I know what you could do. Your mom's got some silver jewelry, right? Earrings and rings and such? Just take those and drop them down the barrel of your Browning. When you shoot it, those things'll do the same thing as a bullet."

I realized then they weren't taking this seriously. Nothing I could say would get through to them.

With a sigh I popped in *Cat People*.

* * *

The next afternoon I was sitting at the top of the stairs, listening to my parents fight.

"I came home early so we could sit and talk," my mom said. "We need to spend some time with just us. It's important that we do that, Wes. Our marriage needs that. Can't you just sit with me for a bit? I'll make you a sandwich."

"I told you. I'm covering for Gellar today. I have to go in early."

"And you're working another double tonight?"

"Yeah. It's good overtime."

"Wes, we don't need the money. I make enough for both of us."

"Look, Babe, I know. Believe me, I know. And hey, this'll all die down once July gets passed us. Everybody takes their vacations in June and July. Once those are out of the way I'll be able to take some time off. If you want, I'll take all this overtime in comp time. I'll build up so many hours off we can stay away for two weeks, if you want. We could take my bike out. Do a little riding down in Galveston, like we used to. Remember that, like when you were doing your residency. Remember…"

The rest faded away into mutterings I couldn't discern.

Then she giggled and said, "Could we? Could we really?"

"Sure," he said. "Now I got to go. Max, come!"

I heard the clatter of Max's claws against our kitchen floor and then the back door slam. After that, the house was quiet.

Then my mom started humming a song I didn't recognize. To me, she sounded unexpectedly happy. She turned on the water at the kitchen sink and I lost the tune over the clatter of dishes getting cleaned.

I thought then what a contradiction my mom was. Here was the smartest person I knew, and certainly the most passionate about learning I'd ever met, and yet she could be lulled into a Cinderella-like state of bliss just at the prospect of some future ride on the back of my dad's motorcycle. She was a wonder to me.

As I sat there contemplating my mom and her many sides, I couldn't help but turn to my own concerns. It was the first night of the full moon, and though my mom had convinced me that the werewolf stuff was just nonsense, I was still very much afraid of what the hairy man would do. My mom had convinced me that calling him a werewolf both aggrandized him, and yet somehow also belittled what he was. He believed himself to be a werewolf, of that I was sure, and that meant that tonight, his terror of fang and claw would begin anew. Death was lurking in the wilderness at the edge of my neighborhood, waiting for the moon to rise. But it also meant that he was just a man. He was no more than I was, or that my dad was. He was, ultimately, something I could wrap my mind around.

I left my perch on the stairs and went to my room. I flipped on the lights and caught sight of something moving out of the corner of my eye. For just a moment, a fraction of a second, I could have sworn I saw Heather Crawford, her throat torn out and her clothes drenched with blood, reaching toward me.

I lurched to one side, hit the lamp on the corner of my desk and knocked it to the floor, where it broke with a loud crack.

I stood there, staring at the corner of the room where I could have sworn she stood, holding my hand over my heart. I felt like it had missed a beat, though now it was thundering against my ribs.

"Mark," my mom called out, "are you okay?"

It took me a second to answer. "Yeah, Mom. I'm fine."

"Did I hear something break?"

"It's all right, Mom. I got it."

But I didn't feel fine. I stood there staring at the corner of my room, and for the longest time I don't think a single coherent thought went through my head. I just stared at the empty corner, trying to catch my breath.

Finally, I had to ask myself the hard questions. Was that really Heather, or my own tattered nerves?

And if it was Heather, what was she trying to tell me?

* * *

Later, I tried to go through my nightly routine of reading a book until I drifted off to sleep. I tried one of my favorites, the Modern Library edition of *Great Tales of Terror and the Supernatural,* but it couldn't hold my interest. I was restless. I went next to my paperback collection of Charles Beaumont's *The Howling Man,* which was another one of my favorites, but even still I had to force my way through three stories before I felt sleep pulling me down.

It was a restless night, but I managed to sleep.

In summer, I was pretty much on my own during the early morning. Dad was on night watch, which meant that he usually didn't make it home until 8 or 9 o'clock in the morning. Mom, on the other hand, was always up well before dawn. She was normally at her practice by 6:30. That left me to sleep late. I was going downstairs just as my dad and Max were dragging in from a night of crime fighting. Both, most of the time, went promptly to bed. That left me with a day empty of parental supervision.

That was how it usually happened, anyway.

But that morning I woke to my mom screaming.

I sat up in bed, trying to figure out what the sound was and where it was coming from. When I realized it was my mom screaming from outside, I ran downstairs. I ran out the front door and skidded to a stop. My mom's car was stopped at the end of the drive, her door open.

In the grass, in a sea of blood, were the dismembered bodies of Billy Steyn, Matt Drake and Lee Johnson.

"Don't, don't, don't come out here," my mom said.

She looked from me to the yard, and I'd never seen her look more terrified, or helpless. She was very close to tears.

As I looked over the yard I saw Billy's body. He was missing a leg and both arms. Near him, hanging off the curb, was a paper grocery bag filled with eggs, a few of them broken and soaking through the bag. I realized then they were going to egg my house when the hairy man got them.

The next moment I realized something else.

The hairy man had been in front of my house.

* * *

My day turned into a circus after that. First the neighbors came out. And I mean all of them. I saw Jeff in the crowd, but his mom had a death grip on his shoulders and he couldn't break loose to talk to me. Then the cops got there. Our yard was blocked off with crime scene tape and a parade of photographers took so many pictures that the flashbulbs nearly burned my eyes out.

And the questions. They never stopped.

My mom and I were separated.

We were put in police cars and driven downtown to the Harris County Sheriff's Office. I saw my mom a few times, but it was always from across a crowded office where the detectives were too busy answering phones or running back and forth to let me talk to her.

Then I was stuck in a dirty little room with a chair and a desk and a trashcan and told to wait, somebody would be with me in a moment or two.

Finally, Detective Travis came in.

I felt relieved to see somebody I knew, though we had never really said more than a few words to each other.

He said, "Hey there, Mark. Had a bit of scare today, huh?"

"Yeah," I said. "I mean, yes sir."

Detective Travis smiled. "It's okay," he said. "Your dad's out there in the office with your mom. I called him."

"Oh," I said. "Can I see him?"

"In a minute. I want to ask you some questions first, if that's okay?"

I nodded, but my gut tightened. My dad was a cop. And I'd made him mad before. Many times actually. I'd even stood up to him, especially lately. But I'd never been the subject of official police questioning. This was something else entirely. I felt the heat rising to my cheeks. I felt my pulse quicken. My hands felt numb.

"Did you know these boys, the ones who got killed?"

"Yes sir."

"You do?" He'd been writing notes to himself on a yellow legal pad, but when I told him that I knew Billy and his gang he put his pen down and seemed to take notice of me all over again. I didn't like the attention. "Do you know their names?"

"Yes," I said, and told him.

"How do you know them? They're all older than you, aren't they?"

"Yes. They're kind of like bullies. They've been picking on me and my friends for a long time now."

"How long?"

I shrugged. "A year or so. Maybe two."

"They pick on you just because, or…"

I shrugged again.

"Mark, talk to me, okay? I know you've been through a bad shock today. Hell, it's been a rough week for you, hasn't it?"

I nodded.

"Mark, I need you to answer me, okay? You can't just shrug or nod. I need you to say something."

Suddenly, I thought of all the times during his interview with Rebecca Hannett that he'd had to ask her to speak her answers out loud and I realized he must have been videotaping our interview.

I looked around, but didn't see a camera. It must have been hidden somewhere, though.

"Yes," I said. "It's been a bad week."

"So why did those boys pick on you?"

I sagged into my chair. Then I told him about the nunchucks incident, and about Billy cornering me in the hall outside my class and about all the times they messed with us at the arcade.

"And this has been going on for about two years you said?"

I nodded. "About that, yeah. I guess that's why they had the eggs."

"What do you mean?"

"You know, to throw them at my house."

"Ah, I get it." He sat back in his chair and studied me for a bit. I tried to look invisible. "Mark," he said.

I looked up.

"What aren't you telling me? I can see by the way you're slouching and the way you won't look me in the eyes that there's something you haven't talked about yet. What's up? You can tell me."

Moment of truth, I thought.

"That day the hairy man attacked me in the Swamp, Billy and his gang were chasing me. He shot me with his pellet gun and when I ran they chased me. That's how I got so far out and found that old house."

He grunted. I couldn't tell from his face whether he was angry or just thinking what to say next. Finally, after like a whole minute of silence, he said, "How come you didn't tell me this when I talked to you last time?"

"Because Billy was already trying to kick my ass every chance he got. The last thing I needed was for him to beat me up again for being a snitch."

"You're not being a snitch for telling the truth."

I sagged further into my chair. "That's what my dad always says."

"Your dad's a good guy."

I nodded.

"But the real issue is this, Mark. First, you don't tell me about Billy and his friends chasing you through the marsh, and the next thing anybody knows, he's dead in your front lawn."

I gawked at him. "I didn't have anything to do with that. It was the hairy man."

"I know you didn't, Mark. No fourteen-year-old kid could rip the arms off of three eighteen-year-old guys. That took a grown man, and a desperate one at that. Did you see the hairy man last night, Mark. Surely you heard something."

"Nothing."

"Nothing at all? Really? Three people were attacked and dismembered in your front yard and you didn't hear anything?"

"I swear, I didn't," I said.

He did that silent treatment again, waiting for me to say something. I didn't. I just sat there staring at the floor.

"Well," he finally said, "you should probably know that we've been searching your neighborhood all day. We haven't found anything."

"That's because he's probably out at that house. He kills by the full moon and goes out there during the daytime."

"By the full moon?"

"Yes," I said, and realized I'd said too much.

"What do you mean about the full moon?"

"Nothing," I said.

"It's not nothing. Mark, if you bring it up it's not nothing. Tell me."

I shook my head, but he had me and we both knew it. I'd let it slip when I wasn't prepared for a lie, and that's always when the truth comes out. I said: "Last month he killed those people during the three days of the full moon. Then nothing until last night, which was also a full moon. He thinks he's a werewolf."

"A what?" he said. A smile tugged at the corner of his mouth.

"A werewolf," I said. I'd gotten kind of excited there for a second, but the look on his face brought me down to earth again. I put my hands in my lap and sulked.

"What makes you think he thinks of himself as a werewolf?"

I didn't say anything.

"Mark?"

"No reason," I said.

"Mark, come on. If you know something, say it."

"I don't know anything," I said. "It's just what my friends and I think."

"Ah," he said. "Okay. Alright, well, you'll tell me or your dad if you think of anything else, won't you?"

I nodded without looking at him.

"Okay," he said. "Come on. Your parents are waiting to take you home."

"But…wait!" I said.

He had started to rise and was already opening the door, but he paused then and looked at me. "Yes?"

"What about the house? Did you guys search the house? That's where he's gonna go."

"We searched it, Mark. We've had officers combing that marsh all day. Dogs too. So far, nothing. Now come on."

He led me out to my parents. Dad was drinking a cup of coffee from a Styrofoam cup. He had an arm around my mom's shoulders. Her face was all red and puffy, like she'd been crying.

"We're all done here," Detective Travis said to my dad. "We're gonna have patrol units working your subdivision all night."

"Thanks, Gene," my dad said.

Travis nodded again. He looked at me. "You'll talk to me or your dad if you remember anything else?"

"Sure," I said. "I mean, yes sir."

Travis smiled. "You're doing fine, Mark."

To my dad he said, "I'll be in touch, okay?"

"Yeah. Thanks."

We left then. My dad had come straight from work when Detective Travis called him, and so he was in his truck. Max was in the back. I asked if I could ride back there with him, but my dad said no. That meant I had to ride with my mom for the thirty minute drive back to Clear Lake.

We didn't say anything until we got back home. But it wasn't to me that my mom finally broke the silence. She went immediately for my dad. "I want you home tonight," she said. "Please."

"Alright," he said, taking a beer out of the fridge. "I'll call in. Gomez should be able to cover my shift tonight." He reached across the kitchen counter and patted my mom's thigh. "Don't worry," he said. He looked at me and smiled. "We're gonna be fine."

* * *

I did feel better with my dad home.

That night, my mom and dad and I shared a bowl of popcorn and watched an episode of *Magnum P.I.* that made my dad laugh because he always laughed at cop shows and then an episode of *Love Boat* that actually got a chuckle or two out of my mom. Max sat behind the couch and I snuck him handfuls of popcorn whenever my dad wasn't looking.

But eventually they sent me off to bed, and I found it nearly impossible to get to sleep. I tried reading and that was a no-go. I even went to the TV room and tried to find something on cable, but there was nothing. Finally I just climbed into bed and watched the ceiling fan spin, hoping I'd drift off but knowing I wouldn't. I was wound too tight for that.

I don't remember what time I gave up on TV, but I do know it was 11:43 when Max started barking. I remember hearing him growl, then let out three rapid-fire barks. I sat up in bed, looked at the clock, and realized that I had almost drifted off to sleep. Then Max started barking again, this time in a continuous, stuttering roar, and I threw back the sheets and ran down the stairs.

My dad was coming out of his bedroom at the same time, wearing only his boxer shorts, his shotgun at the ready.

"Stay back," he said to me, and went to the sliding glass doors that led onto our backyard.

Max was already there at the doors, the hair along his back standing on end, his ears pitched forward, every muscle tensed. He barked again and my dad put his open palm in front of Max's face. "No bark," he said. And Max instantly went quiet.

I came up behind my dad. "What is it? Is it the hairy man?"

"Get down," he said. "Stay low."

My mom came out of the bedroom rubbing her eyes and flipped on the living room light switch.

"Turn that off!" my dad snapped. "Turn it off right now."

The light went out.

I heard my mom say, "Wes, what is it?"

"Shhh," my dad whispered. "Everybody quiet."

He held his shotgun at the ready as he scanned our backyard. Beside him, Max still bristled at the darkness, though he didn't make a sound. I couldn't see anything. I could make out the shapes of shrubs and trees and the little arbor with the covered swing where my mom liked to read her journals when it was cool outside, but nothing else. Nothing moved.

"Mark," my dad whispered, "go into my bedroom and get my radio from the nightstand."

"Yes sir," I said.

I hustled past my mom, who was standing in the doorway to her bedroom, looking lost and frightened, and got my dad's radio.

He took it from me and keyed up.

"Bravo HPD One Ninety-One."

He had turned the volume nearly to zero, so when the dispatcher acknowledged him her voice was barely audible.

"Bravo HPD One Ninety-One, I think you've got some units on special assignment in the Brook Forest subdivision. I need one of them to cover me at one-six-one-one-four Clearcrest. I have a prowler in my backyard."

"Ten-four, Bravo. Any units close?"

"We're right around the corner, Five Double O-Three. Be there in a second."

"Ten-four," the dispatcher said. "All units hold the air until I hear back from Five Double O-Three."

My dad put the radio down on the fireplace mantel.

I said, "Dad…?"

"Shhh. Hold the air."

He was still watching the backyard, his grip tight on the shotgun. Beside him, Max was antsy. He was staring at the yard, ears perked up, but clearly not sensing anything. He looked confused.

I heard the sounds of an engine revving and tires skidding on pavement. That was the Harris County Sheriff's Office on the way to our house, I realized. They were just seconds away.

A car skidded to a stop in front of our house and I heard car doors slam.

"They're here," my dad said. "Everybody stay down."

"Are you going to go out there?" I asked.

"No. Stay down, Mark. My job is to stay here and protect you. I can't do that from out there."

A moment later a pair of Harris County deputies rushed into the backyard, and Max went nuts. He started barking and wouldn't quit.

At the same time there was a flash of movement from above as the hairy man leapt from the roof of our house to the grass, catching the deputies by surprise.

One of them managed to squeeze off a shot, but it went wide and blasted off the top part of one of the boards in our fence. The hairy man let out a howl of rage. And for just a moment, he turned toward our house and seemed to stare into the darkness of our living room.

It looked like he was staring right at me.

Then he turned and ran.

The deputies chased after him, but the hairy man was much faster.

He moved in that same simian crouch I'd seen out at that abandoned house in the Swamp, his arms swinging, his back hunched over forward. He reached the fence and bounded over it in an almost liquid motion that left the deputies far behind. They clambered over, but they were clumsy about it, and it was obvious to me they weren't going to catch him.

One of the deputies, panting and excited, got on the radio.

"Five Double O-Three, I've got one running. Northbound from Clearcrest, headed toward Locke Haven."

"Ten-four," the dispatcher said. "Do I have a unit on Millbridge and Plum Hollow that can respond?"

"Five Double O-Two, we're at Millbridge and Locke Haven, standing by."

"Ten-four," the dispatcher said. "Five Double O-Five, you close?"

"On the way from Plum Hollow and Ledgestone, Five Double O-Five."

I could tell they weren't going to catch him. Already the deputies were sounding winded and confused, with men shouting instructions, sometimes contradictory instructions, back and forth on the radio.

Nobody had a visual on the hairy man.

In the few seconds it had taken him to scurry over our backyard fence, he had melted into the night and lost the cops.

He was gone.

I think my dad realized it too.

He lowered his shotgun and told me to go into the master bedroom with my mom. "You can sleep in the recliner," he said. "Go on, I'll be in soon."

I went, because I trusted my dad with his shotgun, but I couldn't help but think that the hairy man had jumped from our roof.

The backyard part of our roof.

The part right outside my bedroom window.

* * *

I went into my parents' room and saw my mom sitting on the side of the bed.

"Mom, you okay?"

She sniffled and nodded. "I'm fine," she said, and managed a slight chuckle. "Just had a bit of a scare."

"Yeah, you and me both."

That brought another chuckle from her and she turned a little toward me and held up both hands in a gesture for me to come give her a hug, which I did.

"Dad said I could sleep on the recliner tonight."

She nodded and sniffled again. "Good. That's good."

"I love you, Mom."

She squeezed me tighter. "I love you too, Mark. I get so scared thinking about you growing up. I know it's a cliché, but I really do think you've grown up in the blink of an eye. I still remember you crawling around the living room in your diaper, pulling my books down from the bookshelves."

"Mom, come on."

"Hey, I'm your mother. I get to have moments like this if I want to." She huffed, and then released me. "Go on," she said. "Go get some blankets."

I went to the linen closet and got a pillow and some blankets and then tried to make myself comfortable in Dad's old recliner, which wasn't easy because it was hot inside the house and my legs kept sticking to the leather. Finally I gave up on trying to get comfortable and just sat in it, the thinnest blanket I could find draped over my torso. My thoughts turned first to my mom, because I could hear her sobbing in the dark. I could hear the off-balance sway and bump of the ceiling fan, and the mechanical drone of the air conditioner, but over all the noises of our house during the quietest moments of the night, I heard my mom's sobbing.

Listening to it, I wanted to cry myself. I hated feeling this way, so small and helpless, like I had no options. There are very few feelings as bitter and as hateful as being at that stage in life when you realize you're not quite a kid anymore, but then something comes along and stuffs it back in your face that you're not really an adult either. I wanted to have the answers. I wanted to *not* feel helpless. But the truth was I was fourteen and there were actual men, men like my dad and Detective Travis, who knew how to handle this kind of business.

No matter how I looked at it, the situation seemed out of my hands.

I hated it.

But somewhere along the way that hate must have yielded to exhaustion, for I started awake with Max licking my fingertips.

I rubbed Max's head, then sat up.

My dad had clearly not gone to bed, for he was walking into the bedroom, still in his boxers, his shotgun resting on his shoulder.

"Dad?"

"Yeah, Mark."

"Is the power out?"

"Huh? No, it's not light yet."

"What are you doing?"

"I'm getting dressed for work. Max has to qualify on the course today."

"But I thought you were staying home."

I nearly said, "…through the full moon," but managed not to.

"I can't reschedule this. It's state mandated."

"Oh."

"I won't be gone too long," he said. "I should be back by midafternoon. Stay here with your mom, okay? I'll be home well before dinner. When I get home we'll watch a movie or something. Sound good?"

"Yeah," I said. "Sure."

"You didn't sleep much, did you?"

"No, not really."

"That was pretty scary last night."

I looked up in surprise. "You were scared?"

"Sure," he said. "Anytime my family's threatened it scares me."

"I know that," I said. "I meant you, though. When that guy jumped from the roof, that didn't scare you? He was trying to get into the house."

"I know he was. He was right outside your room." My dad stared at me for a moment, then let out a sigh. "Look, Mark, it's okay to be scared. Everybody gets scared. Sometimes, at work, I'll corner a suspect, and there's this moment, there's always that moment, right before you engage the guy. You can see the desperation in his eyes, and you can feel this sick, empty feeling in your gut right before you put your hands on him. That's fear. It never goes away. I felt the same thing last night watching that guy run across the yard. But you can't let your fear rule you. We are gonna get this guy. I promise you that. We're gonna get him, and if I get him first, I'm gonna put a bullet through his head. I promise you that."

I nodded. "Okay."

"Okay, really? You're okay?"

"Yeah," I said. "Thanks, Dad."

He smiled. "It's what I do."

* * *

At 8 a.m. the phone rang.

My mom said, "Hello?" and then stood silently listening for nearly two minutes.

I watched her put her palm on her forehead and slowly drag it down her face. She looked tired.

"Okay," she said. "Yeah, I'll be there in 45 minutes."

I was standing at the entrance to her office.

She said, "I have to go in, Mark. I can't believe this. Grab a book or something and you can come in with me."

"Mom, I don't want to spend all day at the hospital."

"Mark, come on. Don't argue with me, okay? I have to go."

"Then I'll wait here."

"No way. I don't feel comfortable with that."

"Mom, I'll be fine. I'll make myself some nachos and watch *Thundarr the Barbarian* all day."

She paused a moment.

"I don't know."

"Mom, come on. I'll be fine."

She stood there, looking at me. Then I saw her check her watch and I knew I had convinced her.

"Okay," she finally said. "You be good."

"I will."

She kissed my forehead and left.

I went around the empty house, looking out the windows, and the daylight on my face perked me up a little. I thought about the night before, about watching the hairy man jump from the roof right outside my window, and about how small and helpless

I felt while trying to sleep in the recliner in my parents' bedroom, and I started to get angry at myself for the fear I'd shown.

Maybe angry wasn't the right word.

Maybe embarrassed was a better word. Because that was really how I felt. Embarrassed. I looked up to my dad. We fought, we argued, we never really saw eye to eye on anything, especially as I started high school, and yet I never let go of that image of him in uniform, Max at his side, running down the bad guys. He was, always, the hero.

My hero.

And what had I seemed to him?

Nothing but a weakling. A cowering, sniveling, weakling. A child.

He had allowed me a glimpse of the crime scene on the shrimp boat the morning after the storm, and I had paled and been left speechless by that horror. The hairy man overcame me, and only Max's devotion and the police training he had received from my dad had saved me. The hairy man had even tracked me to my home, to my very room, and all I could think to do was to ask my dad about the nature of fear.

I was disgusted with myself.

So I went to his study and I opened the desk drawer where he kept the case file and the *Playboy*. The *Playboy* was gone, but the case file was there. And something more. A new series of pages roughly stuffed on top.

I pulled out the case file and opened it on my dad's desk.

The top page was a grainy looking fax from the Louisiana State Police, addressed to my dad. And below that, in a handwritten scrawl, was a question: *Think this could be your guy?*

A knot formed in my throat as I turned the page.

I saw a black-and-white picture of a young man, in his late twenties, his sandy brown hair a tousled mess. There was dried blood and bruises all over his face. I stared into his eyes and tried to see the deranged, feral intensity I'd seen in the hairy man's eyes, but it wasn't there. The eyes of the man in the picture looked sleepy, like he was exhausted and worn down.

I turned the page and found a typed police report from May 3, 1978.

According to the report, the man had attacked a group of shrimpers in Delacroix, Louisiana. The shrimpers said he tried to bite them, and two of the men were severely injured in the attack before the others could beat him into unconscious submission with a boat hook.

Explains the bruises on his face, I thought.

What I was really looking for was on the last of the new pages.

The hairy man had a name.

James Edward Conlon.

I flipped back to the black-and-white image of the man with the bruised face and tried to picture him as the hairy man. Was it him? Was it really? At first I wasn't sure. But the more I looked, the more certain I became. That was the hairy man. That was as a younger man, perhaps a little more sane, but not by much.

Either way, my devil had a name. And with a name, I had confidence. Finally, I had something I could wrap my mind around.

I thought of what my dad had said. "You can't let your fear rule you."

I wasn't going to let it rule me. I was sick of bullies, and I was sick of cowering in fear. I knew there was one more full moon for the month, and I knew the hairy man, James Edward Conlon, knew where I lived.

He would come back, and he'd be looking for me.

It was the waiting that bred fear. If I was going to take control of my fear, I'd have to take control away from the hairy man.

That meant taking the fight to the hairy man.

That meant going to his house.

* * *

After the incident with my dad's gun he'd hidden the key to his gun cabinet in a different place.

I hadn't bothered to go looking for it.

The anger I'd felt coming off him as he checked the weapon and secured it back in the safe left me quaking in my shoes. The disappointment and betrayal he'd felt, and that he had expressed in his own tacit ways several times thereafter, pushed all desire to shoot the gun ever again straight out of my head.

But things had changed.

Now, I needed that key.

My dad was many things, a great many *good* things. I dare even to say that he was a great man. But he was not especially hard to figure out.

I figured he would never have the key very far from him, for he knew that a gun locked in a safe was the same thing as not having a gun at all if you couldn't get to it. And he had gotten to his shotgun almost instantly the night before when the hairy man jumped off our roof.

That meant the key was by his side of the bed.

I went into my parents' bedroom and searched my dad's bedside table. Nothing but a few magazines and two Joseph Wambaugh books.

Then I remembered a little secret he told me. A lot of police officers tape a handcuff key to the inside of their gun belt, right at the small of their back, just in case they get locked up in their own handcuffs. So I opened the drawer on the bedside table and felt along the underside of the top of the drawer until I found the key.

Then I took it to my dad's closet, opened the safe, and removed his service pistol and a box of ammo.

"Okay, James Edward Conlon," I said. "You want a fight? You're gonna get a fight. Here I come, mother fucker."

* * *

I didn't think about what I was doing until I was on the trail and about to enter the bone yard that surrounded the old abandoned farmhouse. Had it occurred to me before then, I might very well have turned around and headed home with my tail ducked between my legs. As I cleared the trees and saw the house and the sunlight shining on the many, many bones that littered the yard, I realized that I'd crossed my own private Rubicon.

Shooting at that alligator–god, it felt like an eternity ago–the Smith & Wesson had felt cool and comfortable in my hands, a familiar and trusted tool. I felt like I knew the weapon, like it was part of my hand. Though now, as I walked into the bone yard, the gun felt impossibly huge, like more than I could handle.

I wasn't ready for this.

This was a terrible idea.

It was a stupid idea. *Stupid, stupid, stupid.*

But I was committed. So I held the impossibly huge gun out before me and turned a full three hundred sixty degrees, again and again, never stopping, expecting the hairy man to pop out of the house or the surrounding scrub brush and come charging at me.

Nothing moved. The sun was directly overhead, bearing down on me, and as I put up a hand to shield my eyes it occurred to me that it had taken longer to get here than I thought it would. I would have to hurry.

A breeze lifted clouds of dust in the air and carried the fetid stench of decomposing animals my way.

I didn't gag, though.

I was too scared for that.

I wandered up to the porch and looked through the open doorway. There were more bones inside, and what sounded like a man lightly snoring. My hands were sweating and I adjusted my grip on the gun. My face and neck felt hot, my hands cold and numb. I swallowed the lump that had formed in my throat and went inside. The house was empty. No furniture, no pictures on the decaying walls, just trash and bits of the ceiling that had crumbled to the floor. But I could hear the hairy man snoring, and I followed the sound through the empty house, testing every step before I put my weight down just in case the floorboards creaked, taking every breath through my mouth, just like my dad had taught me.

I found him in a corner of one of the back rooms, near the back door. He was sleeping, one arm curled under his head like a pillow.

James Edward Conlon, I thought. My own private devil.

I raised the gun and centered the front sight on his chest. I thought of the gun safety tip my dad repeated every time we went out shooting. Never point your weapon at something you're not willing to destroy. That's exactly what I want to do, I thought. This is the moment I take control of my fear. The hairy man doesn't own it.

I do.

I cocked the hammer back and started to squeeze the trigger, but in the same instant that the hammer cocked, the hairy man's eyes flew open and he scrambled to his feet, faster than I could have imagined. His speed startled me and when the gun went off the shot was wide and blasted a chunk of wood out of the door frame behind him.

The hairy man was out the back door the next instant and I was left holding the gun, staring at an empty doorway, the sound of him running on the packed dirt outside already fading.

"Crap," I said, and stepped out the back door.

He wasn't there.

"Oh no. No, no, no."

I could feel the blood pounding in my ears and I was really starting to sweat. I had to move, I knew that. To stand still would get me killed. So I stepped away from the house and scanned all around me. If he was going to charge me my best chance was to be out in the open, where I'd have time to react.

But he didn't make an appearance.

"Move," I told myself. "Do something."

I stepped around the side of the house and moved to the front.

He wasn't there either.

I continued around, careful to step away from the corners of the house so that I could hopefully see him before he saw me, but he had vanished. I stopped near the front corner of the house where the roof was sagging, held up only by a rotted timber, and forced my breathing to slow. I had to think this through clearly. I needed a plan.

Something snapped behind me and I wheeled around, fumbling to get the gun in front of me.

But there was nothing there.

"Where are you?"

I heard a savage snarl behind me as the hairy man tackled me into the rotting support that held up the roof. The two of us tumbled through it, breaking the rotted wood and crashing onto the deck.

I landed on my back and the hairy man scrambled to get on top of me, his fingernails digging at my throat. I still held the gun, though I couldn't do anything but slap at his arms with it. And still he snarled and raved at me, his eyes full of a feral insanity that turned my blood to ice water.

It was then that the roof collapsed.

I was desperately trying to get his hands from my throat when the roof above us cracked, swayed, and then dropped down on top of us.

The hairy man took most of it on his back and head. He rolled sideways, toward the yard, in a jumble of shattered wood and tarpaper shingles. I hustled to my feet, jumped through the collapsed wall, and ran through the house. Behind me, I heard the hairy man ripping his way through the debris. Then he let out a howl and came charging through the house.

I went out the back door and ran towards the trail, but didn't make it very far. He was on me in no time, knocking me to the ground again. He went for my throat, his fingernails digging into my skin, his grip squeezing tighter and tighter.

I was so terrified, so totally overwhelmed by his snarls and growls, that I only dimly registered the sound of a shot.

Suddenly his hands were gone from my throat and he was rolling off me with a roar of pain.

The next instant I heard a growl and saw Max charging the hairy man. They crashed together in a fury of barks and growls.

Then my dad rushed into the fight, his AR raised high like a club. He brought it down, butt first, meaning to smash in the hairy man's face, but Conlon was quicker. He twisted to one side and the rifle missed its mark. Before my dad could retract the rifle Conlon grabbed it and lashed out with a kick that swept my dad's legs from under him. Conlon swung the rifle around and caught Max in the jaw. I saw blood jet into the air as I rolled over and got to my feet.

The hairy man was standing over my dad, the rifle held high. I saw my dad's hands come up, and the rifle come down with a savage crunch. Max was on his side, tongue hanging loose, his face and flanks spattered with blood. His eyes were closed. The hairy man stood over my dad with the rifle raised high, and as I watched, he brought it down again and again.

I had to act. I had to do something. I ran back toward the house where I'd dropped my dad's pistol. The hairy man must have heard me for he turned and walked toward me, his eyes full of hate. I reached the jumbled mass of wood and tarpaper shingles and looked all around for the gun.

The collapsed roof had formed a sort of shell over it. I tried to reach through the broken timbers but it was just out of reach.

Behind me, the hairy man snarled.

I chanced a look back over my shoulder and he smiled with a sick, depraved look in his eyes.

I jammed my hand back into the hole of wood and shingles, desperately trying to reach the gun.

It was still out reach.

"God damn it!" I screamed, and threw my shoulder into the pile of debris.

It collapsed beneath me and the next instant the pistol was right in front of my face. I picked it up, turned, and pointed it at the hairy man.

He stopped, and for just a moment, just one horrible moment, I thought I saw the veil of madness lift from his face.

Then he snarled and lunged for me.

I fired a shot.

The hairy man stopped. There was a fresh wound in his chest, a spreading teardrop of blood oozing from the hole. He looked at me, and I thought I saw fear in his eyes. And, maybe, a trace of human understanding of the end of all flesh, a realization that he'd just been dealt a mortal blow.

But it was gone so fast I'll never truly know, for the next instant his eyes narrowed and he leaned forward in a crouch and sprang toward me.

I fired three more times before he dropped face down in the dirt.

I stood there for a long moment, the gun held level at empty air. I was stunned by what I'd just done. I felt no triumph, no remorse, only a cold numbness spreading outward from my chest.

I didn't move until my father groaned.

I dropped the weapon and I went to him. His face was battered. His lips had burst. His nose was flattened and almost black with blood. But his eyes were still strong. He stared up at me for a long moment, as though questioning if this was real, and then he threw his arms around me.

With a lot of effort, I helped him to his feet.

He went to the hairy man's side and put his fingers on the man's neck to check for a pulse. "He's dead," he said. He looked at me. "You got him. It's over."

I nodded. It was over. There didn't seem to be anything more to say.

He scooped up his service revolver and his AR and we went over to check on Max. He was hurt and whimpering, and he had some bleeding bite marks on his face, but it didn't look like anything was broken.

"Come on, boy," my dad said. "Up!"

Max climbed to his feet, in pain, but still moving.

I said, "How did you know I'd be here?"

"Your mom came home and you weren't there. When I got home I checked for the key to the gun cabinet and it wasn't where it was supposed to be. You left it in the lock. As soon as I saw that the rest wasn't hard to put together. She's scared out of her mind for you, by the way."

"I'm sorry," I said.

We walked toward the trail, back toward home. He was limping.

"You mind if I ask you why?" he said.

I stopped and stared at him. "Because of you."

"Me? What in the world made you think I wanted you to do this?"

"Because of what you said about fear. You said I can't let my fear control me. So I didn't. I took control of my fear, just like you said."

He looked thoroughly confused. "Mark," he said with a heavy sigh. "I do believe you are gonna be the death of me."

* * *

After the fight with the hairy man, my dad and I met a team of deputies from the Harris County Sheriff's Office at the entrance to the Swamp and one of them took me home to my mom while Max and my dad led the others back out to the old house where the hairy man lay dead.

When I walked in the front door, the deputy right behind me, my mom came running out of the kitchen, tears streaming down her face. She saw me, and I thought she might collapse right there in the entryway. Instead she let a long, labored groan of relief and then scooped me up in her arms. I thought she had hugged me tight that night we took shelter from the storm in our hall closet, but that was nothing compared to this. And I didn't care. For all the world, I didn't care. I was home.

When at last she gave up the hug she held me at arm's length and looked me over. I think I gave her another scare with the way I looked. I was covered in sweat and grass and bits of wood and a lot of dried blood. She could barely speak for shaking.

"Are you hurt?" she asked.

"I tried to rub my shoulder where I'd hit the porch column on the old house, but a sudden stab of pain shot from my joint and up my neck. I gave it up, wincing. "Shoulder's kinda stiff," I said.

"Oh baby," she said. She hugged me again. The pain was still with me, but I didn't care. Then she looked into my eyes and said, "Why did you do this? You had me so scared." She sniffled and wiped the tears from her eyes with the back of her hand. "I've never been that scared in my life."

"I'm sorry, Mom."

She started to cry and I did too.

Finally the deputy told my mom that I was needed at their Homicide Office, that Detective Travis needed to get my statement.

"Can I come with him?"

"Yes ma'am, Detective Travis said that would be okay."

"One minute," I said.

I pointed at my hip and said, "I still have my dad's service revolver. I need to put it in his gun safe."

The deputy was a giant of a man, and old, past fifty, with thin white hair and a chest like a keg of beer. His gaze drifted from the bulge under my shirt to my face. I couldn't really figure the look on his face, whether he was mad at me for the delay I was causing or at himself for not realizing the gun was there.

"Yeah, that's fine," he said. "But do it quickly please."

"Yes sir," I said, and ran for my dad's closet.

Once I had the gun safe open I slid the weapon out of my jeans, opened the cylinder, and ejected the spent shell casings into my hand. I thought back to the day my dad had come home and found me in this very spot, putting the weapon back. I remembered how he'd checked the weapon over, how he'd muttered to himself the gun safety rules I'd heard so many times before, and found myself muttering those same rules over now as I visibly and physically checked to ensure I had an empty weapon. It felt like I was paying a penance somehow. Like I was finally giving my dad the respect I'd been unable to offer up before. At that moment, for the first time in my life, I think I finally realized the power built into a gun, and what it meant to use one.

* * *

It was past two in the morning when Detective Travis put the cap back on his pen and said, "Well, I guess that about covers it. How you doing, Mark? You look tired."

I was. I felt exhausted. I wanted to crawl into my bed and sleep for days.

"I'll be alright," I said. "Where are my parents?"

"Your dad's been done for a while now. He's out in the hall with your mom. Come on. I'll take you there."

I followed him out to the hall. My parents were down at the far end, near the exit doors, their arms wrapped round each other. My mom looked so comfortable in his arms. I started to call out to them, but Detective Travis put a hand on my shoulder to quiet me.

"They fight a lot, don't they?" he said.

That caught me off guard, and my first reaction was to get angry. What business was that of his? But the look on his face wasn't mean or cruel. Quite the opposite actually. I got the sense he was trying to tell me something.

"Yeah, they fight," I said. Then I added defensively, "Everybody fights."

"True. But it's different for cops and their wives."

"What do you mean?"

He turned a patient smile on me. For a moment I thought he might rough up my hair. Thank God he didn't.

"When I was a cadet at the Sheriff's Academy, there was this PT instructor who used to love to make us do push ups out on the lawn every time it rained. This one day I was there doing push ups, the rain coming down on my back, soaking my uniform, when this instructor comes strolling through our ranks carrying an umbrella. I remember he said, 'Why did you idiots want to become cops? Three things will happen to you in the first year you wear a badge. You will buy a truck. You will buy a house. And you will get divorced. You are all a bunch of stupid mullets if you think you can beat those odds. Just quit right now. It'd be easier on you if you just found a woman you hated and gave her half your pension. That way you wouldn't have to live with the misery of a divorce.'" Travis smiled to himself, like he was looking back on a fond memory. "I hated that man," he said. "But he was right. Being a cop pretty much destroys any chance you've got of living a happy homelife." He pointed down the hall. "But your dad and your mom, I think they're one of the lucky couples that get to make it. If she's stayed with him this long, I think she's in for the long haul. God help her though. It's tough being married to an ass. And believe me, every cop's wife eventually discovers she's married to an ass. Maybe a noble ass, but an ass just the same."

"My dad is not an ass," I said.

He smiled. "I know he's not. Not to his boy. Not to the world. Your dad's a good man. What I'm talking about is different from all that."

One thing I always hated about adults was that condescending you'll-understand-one-day smile. If he'd been a kid my age I would have accused his parents of being a separate species.

Instead, I offered him a bland smile.

"Go on," he said, and gestured toward my parents with a nod of his head. "You guys will be just fine."

* * *

Max was our big worry in the days after our encounter with the hairy man. He'd whimpered and whined most of the way out of the Swamp, and yet, when faced with coming home with me or going back out into the Swamp with my dad and the deputies, he hadn't hesitated. He'd spent the entire day with my dad. But that night, when we came home, we found him whimpering in pain and drooling inside his crate.

Back in 1983, the Houston Police Department only had one on-call veterinarian for their service animals, and it had taken nearly four hours to get him on the phone.

But eventually we did.

He had a broken rib. The vet treated him, and he came home to us with bandages wrapped around his chest. We had instructions to change out the bandages every morning and every night, and to monitor him in case he tried to bite them off, but after three days he'd sort of accepted the bandages and the pain didn't seem to bother him as much.

My dad was home the whole time, and I think that more than anything helped Max with his recovery. I know he whined every time my dad went out the door, like he was afraid his master was going off to work without him.

But he got better.

I was thankful for that.

About a week later, this was around lunch, I went into the kitchen and found my parents laughing. They each had a glass of wine in their hands and there was a plate of crackers and soft, gooey cheese on the counter behind my dad.

"Hey," I said, nodding at them.

My mom glanced from me to my dad. Dad said, "You going somewhere?"

I'd spent most of that morning hanging out with Max and reading Robert McCammon's *The Night Boat*, still in my PJs. Now I was dressed in jeans, sneakers, and an Iron Maiden t-shirt that I bought when I caught them at the Astrodome the year before.

"I want to go see Alan," I said.

My mom stiffened. My dad frowned. "You think that's the best thing to do?" he asked.

"I don't know," I said honestly. "I don't know what to do, Dad. But I know I can't sit around and do nothing, you know?"

He nodded slowly. "Yeah, I'm learning that about you."

I nodded.

"You'll tell me how Jeanne is doing?" my mom asked.

"Mrs. Crawford…uh, yeah."

"What time will you be back?"

I shrugged. "I don't know. I guess, you know, that depends."

"If you get back in time we could go to the Cajun House for dinner."

"Really?"

"Yeah," my dad said. "Sounds great."

The Cajun House did a crawfish boil that was out of this world. They put wax paper on your table and then the waiter came out with this big stew pot of steaming crawfish and corn and red potatoes and Andouille sausage and spilled it out across the wax paper. It was my all-time favorite restaurant.

"Go on," my dad said. "Tell us how it goes, okay?"

Ten minutes later I was knocking on Alan's door, and I realized as I took my hand away that I was feeling the same sort of fear I'd felt as I entered the clearing to shoot the hairy man. I had just made a long bike ride through my neighborhood without remembering an inch of it. I was so focused on what I was doing that time and distance had slipped by and I hadn't noticed. And now I stood on my friend's doorstep, much as I had stood on the hairy man's doorstep, with no idea of what was to come, and even why I thought this was a good idea.

Alan's mom answered the door. She looked like the last few weeks had drained the life out of her. She wasn't wearing any makeup, and her face was haggard and gray. Not quite old, but getting there. Her eyes were vacant. I found it impossible to hold her stare. I think it was her hair that alarmed me most, though. It had been jet black for as long as I'd known her, but it had turned a lackluster brown, gray in places, and it stuck out like wires from the back of her head.

For a moment I don't think she recognized me, but then she forced a smile and said, "Hello Mark."

"Hello Mrs. Crawford." An uncomfortable silence passed between us. "Is Alan home?"

"He's upstairs," she said. "In his room."

"Oh. Um, would it be okay if I went up to see him?"

"I don't know, Mark. He hasn't been doing very well lately. He's so sensitive."

"I…I just want to speak with him. I promise I won't be long."

She looked down at the ground, and I got this feeling I was watching a woman so mired under grief and exhaustion that she could simply tune me out and forget she was standing in her open front door wearing only her nightgown and slippers.

For a moment, I almost turned away.

But then she said, "I heard about what you and your dad did, on the news."

I didn't speak. I waited instead.

"Thank you," she said. "I go to church, Mark. Did Alan ever tell you that?"

"Uh, yes ma'am."

"I'm shocked that I can put this into words, but I'm glad you killed that man." She sucked in a breath and put a hand over her mouth. "That's awful of me to wish a man dead, but I am glad. I wished him dead and then he was dead. I feel so ashamed."

I opened my mouth but no words came out. I honestly had no idea what to say. The woman in front of me was tearing herself apart with guilt and grief and things I probably couldn't even put words to, and yet here was a grown woman sobbing without shame in front of me, even putting her arms around my shoulders so that I could feel her tears on my face, and I had no idea what to say.

"I'm sorry," I said, putting my arms clumsily over her shoulders. "I don't know what to do. I don't know what to say. Heather was the coolest girl I ever knew."

She separated from me then and stared at me, the tears lingering on her cheeks.

For a moment I thought she'd tell me to go, but she didn't.

She said: "She was, wasn't she?"

"The coolest," I said.

"She used to tell me about babysitting you. Did you know that?"

"No," I said. "I didn't."

"She said you were such a smart kid. She said you knew everything there was to know about horror movies and scary books."

I couldn't help but smile. I remembered watching *Trilogy of Terror* with her, and the way she'd retreated to the kitchen as Karen Black bared her terribly sharp teeth and stabbed the floor with a kitchen knife as she waited for her shrew of a mother to arrive, the Zuni warrior in possession of her soul. It was the longest I'm-going-for-a-drink-of-water I can remember.

I couldn't help but laugh.

"She was cool," I said.

Mrs. Crawford went blank at that, like the memories of her daughter threatened to consume her, body and soul. I thought for sure this time would be like all the other times and she would close the door in my face.

But she didn't. She took a step back and let the door hang open wide.

"He's upstairs," she said.

"Oh, okay, thank you."

I took a step inside and gave her a glance. She nodded in reply and I started up the stairs with ice in my gut.

It took Alan a moment to answer my knock on his door. I could hear him moving around in there, and then finally he opened the door.

He just stared at me.

I said, "Alan..."

"Go away, Mark. I want to be left alone."

"Alan, please," I said. "Please, let me talk to you."

He still had a hand on the door, and for a moment I thought he might close it in my face, but then his hand fell away and he walked to the center of his room and turned around to face me. Our rooms couldn't have been more different. Mine was walled with books, except of course for the poster of Phoebe Cates in that red bikini from *Fast Times at Ridgemont High*, which dominated the spot above my bed. Alan's room was devoted to his two great loves, music and movies. He had an acoustic guitar on a stand in the corner, and his beloved trumpet resting on his desk. There were few books, though. Instead, he'd covered his walls in movie posters, everything from the German version of *The Thing* to the fantastic cityscapes of *Blade Runner* to a cartoonish rendering of *The Best Little Whorehouse in Texas*. I stepped into the room and glanced around and said, "I saw a *Conan the Barbarian* poster at the mall the other day."

He just stared at me.

"How you been, Alan? I've missed hanging out with you."

Again, no response.

"Alan, are we still friends?" I couldn't endure more of his silence so I hurried on, just filling the space between us with the first thing that came to mind. "I want to be, but I just don't know how to reach you anymore. I want to. Alan, please, come on. Talk to me."

I waited.

Nothing.

At that moment I felt stupid for coming. And truth be told I felt angry at him for his silence. "Alright," I said. "I'm gonna go, I guess. This was a mistake. I shouldn't have bothered you."

I turned to the door.

"Wait," he said.

I turned around.

"I saw what you did on the news."

I nodded, waiting for more.

"You're a real hero, aren't you?" His tone was suddenly venomous.

"I'm no hero," I said guardedly.

"But you killed him. The police didn't do it. Max didn't do it. The Community Watch didn't do it. Hell, your own father didn't do it. You did."

"I was scared," I said. "The whole time."

"Yeah?"

"Yeah."

He stepped in close. Too close for my comfort, but I didn't back away. "You think it'll bring her back?"

It sounded like he was taunting me.

"What? No, of course not."

His smile turned cruel. I tried to back away from him, but he rushed me. He threw three fast punches at my face and I tumbled over backwards trying to get out of the way.

He fell on me, throwing one blind punch after another.

"You think it'll bring her back?" he screamed at me. "Do you?" Another punch. "Do you?"

I held up my hands to deflect the blows. It did little to stop them. He went on screaming as he hit me, but I couldn't understand him at that point. Alan was completely gone. He just kept punching, one blow after the other. His face was twisted into a grotesque mask of rage, white bits of spit on his lips. There was blood on his hands. My blood.

"I want her back," he said, and threw another punch.

I felt like I was about to black out, and I knew I had to do something.

"Get off," I said, and rolled to one side. He tried to stay on top of me, but I heaved one knee up and it tilted him off balance enough for me to throw him toward the bed. He landed with one arm underneath it so that when he tried to get back to his feet his shoulder was wedged under the bed.

It gave me time to get back up.

He got up too.

I touched my fingers to my nose and they came away bloody. I glanced at the mirror above his dresser and saw that he'd busted my lip up pretty good. I was probably going to have a black eye, maybe two.

"I want her back," he said. Suddenly all the wind seemed to go out of his sails. He deflated right in front of me. His shoulders drooped and he started to cry. "I want her back."

There was a furious burst of knocking on his bedroom door. "Is everything okay in there?" his mom yelled. "What's going on? Open this door."

I waited for Alan to answer

"Alan?" she called out.

I looked at him. He was shaking all over.

"Yeah," he said then, and despite his trembling, his voice sounded remarkably level and calm. "We're fine," he said. "I slipped."

I lowered my fists. "We're fine, Mrs. Crawford," I said.

"Okay," she said. She sounded uncertain, but soon enough we heard her footsteps going down the stairs.

He met my gaze, and all his ferocity was gone.

The tears kept coming though.

"You look a mess," he said.

"So do you."

"Yeah, well," he said with a shrug, "it's been that kind of summer."

THE END

Joe McKinney has been a patrol officer for the San Antonio Police Department, a homicide detective, a disaster mitigation specialist, a patrol commander, and a successful novelist. His books include the four part Dead World series, Quarantined, Inheritance, Lost Girl of the Lake, The Savage Dead, Crooked House and Dodging Bullets. His short fiction has been collected in The Red Empire and Other Stories and Dating in Dead World. In 2011, McKinney received the Horror Writers Association's Bram Stoker Award for Best Novel. For more information go to
http://joemckinney.wordpress.com.

www.ingramcontent.com/pod-product-compliance
Lightning Source LLC
Chambersburg PA
CBHW050524260626
47157CB00004B/1463

* 9 7 8 1 9 4 0 1 6 1 1 2 9 *

Deadly Passage

JournalStone's DoubleDown Series, Book III

By

Sanford Allen

JournalStone
San Francisco

JournalStone books may be ordered through booksellers or by contacting:

JournalStone
www.journalstone.com
www.journal-store.com

ISBN: 978-1-940161-12-9 (sc)
ISBN: 978-1-940161-29-7 (hc – limited edition)
ISBN: 978-1-940161-13-6 (ebook)

Library of Congress Control Number: 2013951062

Printed in the United States of America
JournalStone rev. date: December 6, 2013

Cover Design: Paul Vaughn
Cover Art: Alfredo Lopez Jr.
Edited by: Elizabeth Reuter

For Tracey

Deadly Passage

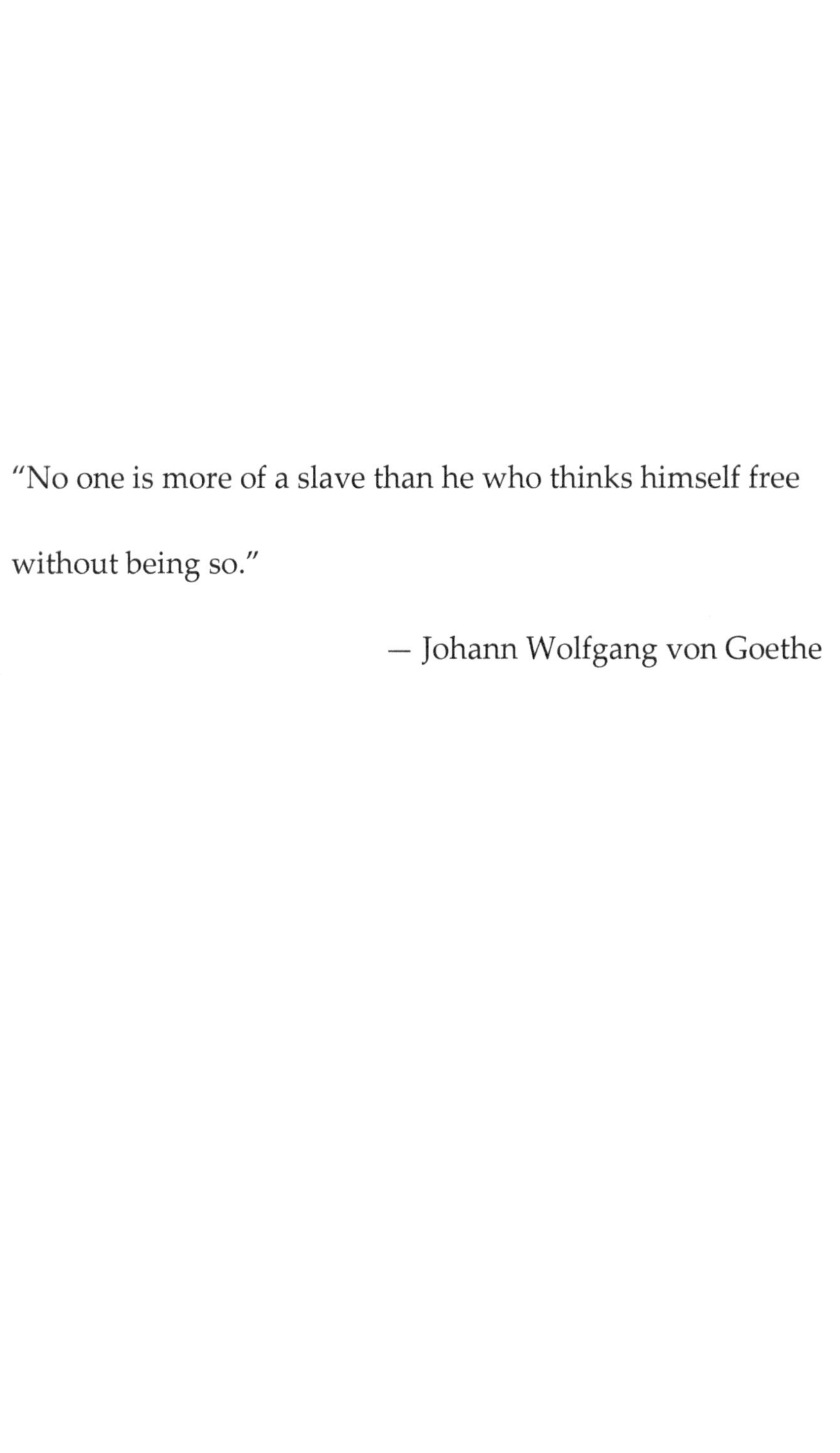

"No one is more of a slave than he who thinks himself free without being so."

— Johann Wolfgang von Goethe

Deadly Passage

The beast climbed down its gnarled tree by cover of night. It moved in an awkward crouch through the tall yellow grass, for it had never truly adapted to walking on land like the humans it hunted.

It slunk between tangled copses, moving ever closer to the shore, a place it had never hunted before. Its old grounds had become fallow.

Humans once wandered below the branches of its tree looking for fallen nuts and berries, easy prey as it swung down on hooked feet. Sometimes, travelers even curled up to sleep at the tree's roots. The beast would descend upon them, put its mouth to theirs and suck away their breath and blood before they could wake.

But the humans it hunted no longer appeared among the trees. They were gone from their smoldering villages, led away by other humans armed with blades that glinted under the bright sun and long sticks that threw fire.

The dead they left in their wake rotted in the sun and provided little sustenance. Most of their blood had already drained into the sand.

The beast's prowl through the tall grass led it to a hill that looked down upon the shore. Waves crashed against an immense hut stronger than any the beast had seen before.

Rather than wood and reeds, the hut was built of stones laid one upon another. Human men with fire sticks walked along its

walls. These men were pale as glistening grubs. They looked as if they had already been emptied of blood.

A wooden canoe floated in the ocean nearby. Like the stone hut, it was larger than any other human-made thing the beast had seen. It was big enough to hold a village, and indeed, several huts were built upon it. Leafless trees taller than any in the beast's woods grew from the middle.

Intrigued, the beast braved sunrise. It preferred not to be on the ground when humans' light vision returned, but the grass on the hill was high and it shielded the beast well.

More men milled around the canoe's huts. Like those of the stone hut, these men were pale, bloodless and unappetizing. Some climbed in the leafless trees, as if looking for fruit along the neat, even branches. They draped long sheets of white cloth from the branches like robes drying in the sun.

The beast caught a familiar smell—that of healthy, brown-skinned humans with blood pumping through their hearts.

A line of these men and women, more than the beast had seen in a long time, shuffled from the stone hut. They descended toward the floating village. They were bound at the wrists and ankles, shoved along by the bloodless ones.

The sun had begun to slip low in the sky by the time the last of the brown-skinned humans disappeared into the floating village. Their smell was still strong.

The beast's hunger made it careless. As it moved closer, it realized one of the pale humans with fire sticks had heard its movement. The man raised his weapon and stepped into the tall grass, craning his long pale neck for a better look.

He moved in the slow, clumsy manner of his kind, feet noisily crunching rock and dried plants. Even though his eyes gazed in the beast's direction, he saw nothing.

The pale man did not even have time to use his weapon before the beast was on him, opening his throat with a claw. Hidden in the yellowed sea of grass, it lapped up the blood that flowed from the man's twitching body. His blood was far more appetizing than his pale skin suggested.

The beast, rejuvenated by the taste of human blood, climbed down the cliff and hid among the rocks. Sated and strong, it could easily scale the wood walls of the big canoe.

Once inside, it would eat better than it had in many rains.

* * *

A leaden sky settled low over the *Lombard*.

Low enough, it seemed to George Bell, that the brig's mainmast might penetrate the dark clouds and unleash drenching rains.

He wondered if those rains would delay the bloody spectacle he and the rest of the crew were assembled to witness.

"Bell," the mate, Ned Bevan, called. "Fetch Captain Pearson so we can begin." He uncoiled the whip he kept tucked under his belt.

Bell nodded and headed for the captain's cabin, hoping the slave's flogging would commence without him. It was a scene he would see play out many times during the voyage, and one he tried to avoid when he could.

After serving twice before on the Middle Passage, Bell was not squeamish when it came to the cruelties of the trade. But as the only black among the *Lombard*'s crew of twelve, he still felt uneasy watching such punishment meted out.

He was here for money and money alone, and the pursuit of money meant selling a bit of one's soul and sanity. If he had learned anything since being run away from the arms Alice Dryden, it was that only with money—and the land it bought—could a freeman earn respect.

Bell rapped on the door of the captain's quarters and Pearson appeared, blue jacket hanging loose over a frame so broad it made his head seem too small for his body.

The captain furrowed his brow.

"What is it then, Mr. Bell?"

"Mr. Bevan is dispensing punishment to one of the slaves. He asked I summon you."

Pearson buttoned his jacket as he followed Bell to the bow. The entire crew of twelve, light for a brig, circled the foremast. Pearson preferred to travel light, maximizing speed and minimizing expenditure on wages.

"What is the nature of this Negro's insubordination?" Pearson asked as he stepped into the ring of sailors. His face was an impassive mask. To Bell, he seemed to carry an air of dignity none of the drunkards, thugs and misfits that made up his crew could muster.

"He acted up during feeding time, sir," Bell said.

"The animal threw his own shit at one of my men," Bevan corrected curtly. He flipped the whip, as if in practice. Its braided lash moved across the deck like a slithering blacksnake. A smile spread to Bevan's thin lips. "Earned himself fifteen lashes."

Pearson nodded. "Mr. Bell, why don't you do the duty? Since you're cut in with a full share this voyage, I think it's appropriate you take part in the discipline."

Bell's stomach flipped and his mouth went dry. The lash was a punishment he had endured only once before winning his freedom—when he'd made the mistake of striking another servant on the sugar plantation in a dispute. He felt sick even thinking of inflicting it on someone else.

"Yes sir," Bell said. He reached for the whip, willing his hand not to shake. Although Pearson treated him well, Bevan and most of the whites in the crew seemed to watch him with predatory intensity for any sign of weakness or insubordination. "My pleasure."

But Bevan didn't offer up the whip. His eyes stayed focused on the slave lashed to the mast. "All respect due, Captain, I'd rather not turn this over. This savage's display warrants stern punishment as a warning to the others." He jerked his head toward Bell, barely suppressing a sneer. "Not a clumsy flailing at the hands of a novice."

"Very well," Pearson said. "Just make sure Bell handles it next time there's need for punishment."

Bell shrunk from the captain's side. Sure he was out of the officers' gaze, he exhaled relief.

Pearson turned to the crew and held up his chin, as he often did before summoning an appropriate verse from the Bible or one of his books on maritime law. Bell suspected which verse was likely to follow.

"Slaves, obey your earthly masters with deep respect and fear," the captain bellowed. "Serve them sincerely as you would serve Christ. Ephesians 6:5."

He'd guessed right.

Bell wondered why Pearson thought the African could understand a single word he'd said. Or, indeed, why he thought that any of the ruffians in the crew would seek Biblical sanction before flogging a slave.

The captain's constant quoting from the Good Book, Bell decided on his first voyage with the *Lombard,* amounted to self-justification.

Pearson waved a hand. "Carry on with the punishment, Mr. Bevan."

The whip's first crack sounded loud as a musket shot, its fall rupturing the lanky African's bare back. His body recoiled as much as his bonds allowed. He dangled from the mast, toes barely touching the deck, wrists bound to pegs driven into the wood.

A trickle of blood rolled down the man's bare buttocks and thighs, mingling with the saltwater pooled on the *Lombard*'s deck.

Bell turned his head. Phantom pain stung his shoulders as the lash landed again.

Beyond the brig's low railing, the blue-green Atlantic rocked in slow, foamy swells. The sea, open and wide, had promised free movement and endless possibilities for Bell, a balm for his two decades of captivity. For the slave tied to the mast and for his thirty-nine fellows crammed below deck, however, the same sea promised a lifetime in chains.

The whip cut the air again and the African's whimpering transformed into a high, wailing scream. Laughter erupted from several of Bell's white shipmates and he turned his eyes back to the deck. The oafish red-bearded boatswain, Follett, guffawed as if he'd heard a particularly bawdy joke. He bared a sparse collection of teeth, some gray as the clouds above, others nearly black.

Bevan brought back his whip to deliver another lash. Red droplets the size of dollar coins dotted his white sleeve. The slave hung in his bonds, eyes closed, bottom lip quivering. His back looked like a burst melon.

"You've given him enough," Pearson said, dusting his palms together. "Insubordination or no, I don't want to lose a slave to his wounds a week into the return trip."

Bevan lowered the whip, face slack with disappointment. He coiled the leather cord and wrung it with both hands like a wet shirt. Blood rained on the deck.

"Throw saltwater on the nigger's back and take him below," he ordered. Follett ambled to the mast and began cutting the man down.

Relieved the ordeal was over, Bell turned to busy himself below deck.

"It bothers you to watch that, doesn't it, Mr. Bell?" Pearson asked him.

"I know what this job entails."

"I suppose you do. Three times out is more than most men can stand, even most whites."

Another crewman joined Follett in hoisting down the African. He hung loose in their arms, eyes closed, face wrenched into a tight mask of pain.

"Throwing his own feces," Pearson said, shaking his head. "Do you understand the Africans?"

"I understand a few words of Twi," Bell said. "What I've learned from the fort bailiffs. Trade things mostly."

"No," Pearson said. "I mean understand their minds. You and the Creole traders I've encountered are civilized Negroes. These are a brutish race unto themselves."

Bell shrugged. "My family is from Barbados, lived and worked with whites back to my great-grandfather's day. I suppose that makes us different from saltwater slaves."

"Black or white, you're the best carpenter I've worked with. You should rethink your decision not to go out again. Plenty of rot in this old brig needs your attention."

"You've been more than fair, sir, what with cutting me in on the bonus this time," Bell said. "But I'm done after this. I want a life on dry land."

"If there's anything the colonial fleet taught me, it was to punish the insubordinate, reward the loyal and guide both with good scripture." Pearson drew a deep breath, as if the ocean's briny scent rekindled memories of his service. "Assuming you earn your bonus, you'll have good stock to choose from. I'd wager the majority survive the trip."

"I think the tall one might be a prize pick," Bell said.

Pearson looked surprised. "The one with the scars cut into his head? He's got a strong back for the fields, but I doubt anyone would want that lumbering beast in his house."

"He speaks English already," Bell said. "The bailiffs told me he'd traded with them before he was captured by a rival tribe."

"I'm surprised he has the temperament for trade. Judging by the scars, he's one of the northern tribesmen. I normally refuse to take any of them. They're a headstrong bunch prone to suicide and mutiny. That bastard Dutchman slipped him in under my nose."

"I suspect he'll fetch a good enough price," Bell said.

"Enough to buy that farm of yours, eh?"

"I aim to work only for myself."

"You're ambitious as any white man, Bell." Pearson's mouth hitched in a smug smile. "Until we make port, though, remember where your loyalty lies."

"It lies with you, sir," Bell said. "It lies with the *Lombard*."

The captain nodded once and made toward his cabin.

Follett pitched a bucket of saltwater. Its froth carried the slave's spilled blood over the side of the ship.

* * *

That night, the dense gray clouds that canopied the *Lombard* unleashed a fierce storm. Squalls the height of plantation houses buffeted the brig, washing into its lower decks. Skeletal fingers of lightning jabbed the black sky.

Bell swayed through the night in his hammock, catching little sleep as the vessel rocked over the waves.

In the morning, he descended the stairs into the slave hold, boots sloshing in the ankle-deep water the storm left behind. William Dowd, a young sailor Bell suspected had been pressed into duty to pay off tavern debts, climbed down behind him.

Forty Africans huddled in their soaked berths, stacked like spoons in two double-tiered shelves. Their naked, drenched bodies shivered in the chill morning air. Their eyes followed Bell and Dowd as they moved through the cramped hold, ducking their heads under the ship's support timbers.

Bell dipped a dented ladle into the feeding bucket he'd lugged down the stairs. He slopped a wad of kankey into the first slave's outstretched hands. The corn gruel dripped down the woman's manacled wrists and between her clenched palms. She buried her face in the slop, gulping it down.

Bell walked the portside aisle sloshing a spoonful into each set of outstretched hands. The sickly-sweet smell of overcooked corn and palm oil drifted up from the bucket.

Dowd, long brown hair tied back, slipped his red neckerchief over his nose and mouth and followed Bell, carrying out his even less pleasant duty. He jammed a wooden hoe onto each shelf, sliding out coils of excrement and depositing them into a stinking slop bucket of his own.

Just a week offshore, and the hold already reeked. The smell of compressed, fearful humanity—of their sweat, piss and shit—would only grow more acrid on the voyage. No matter how often the crew raked with shit hoes, swabbed the berths with vinegar or burned buckets of pitch, the nauseating odor would not go away.

Soon, Bell knew, it would spill topside and cloak the boat like a dense, choking cloud. It would seep into the crew's clothes, root in their hair and find its way into the food they ate. The only consolation: it would become so omnipresent they'd eventually cease to notice.

But that time had not yet arrived.

He readied a ladleful for the starboard row's last slave, the tall, scarred man he'd mentioned to Pearson. The broad-

shouldered northern tribesman raised himself on his elbows. His shaved head, marked with three identical lines on either side, almost touched the top of the shelf above.

"Time to eat," Bell said, hoping to hear the man's English.

The giant met Bell's gaze but said nothing. His dark eyes smoldered with an unbroken intelligence. He did not immediately extend his hands like the others. Instead, he kept them pressed to the berth, palms down.

Bell sensed that the African wanted to make *him* wait. Perhaps Pearson had been right. The man was stubborn.

"Should I move on?" Bell asked, again trying to solicit a response. The man didn't speak, nor did he look away. He slowly extended a hand twice the size of Bell's.

Bell dripped kankey into the outstretched palm and dropped the ladle back into his bucket with a hollow thunk. The man didn't move to feed himself until Bell turned.

Most of the slaves had been broken by weeks in the fort by the time the *Lombard* loaded them aboard. That the tribesman showed such determination spoke either to his strength or cunning—perhaps both.

Bell crossed to the other row of shelves. The slaves' black iron bonds rattled as they stretched out hopeful hands. He moved down the line, slathering palms with gruel, until he reached the two curled at the end of the berth.

Neither moved when he banged the ladle into the bucket. They slumped against each other, arms stretched against the irons that anchored them in place.

The raw red gashes across one's narrow back revealed him as the slave Bevan flogged the day before. He nudged the man. His head rocked sideways, jaw opening into a puddle of water left by the previous night's storm. A single droplet of blood—deep red, almost black—dripped from his mouth into the pooled saltwater.

The African's dead eyes seemed locked on a narrow gap perhaps six inches wide where the hold's wood planks fell just short of the top deck.

* * *

The two dead men sprawled on the deck looked as if they had been rolled in campfire ash. Bell, standing among the assembled crew, hadn't fully realized the dead Africans' lack of color in the dark, cramped hold.

Pearson thrust his hands into the pockets of his blue jacket and regarded the bodies. "What do you make of it, Doctor? Smallpox?"

Josiah Hicks, the *Lombard*'s surgeon, puffed at his thin ivory pipe. The stream of earthy-smelling smoke didn't mask the reek of rum that seemed to soak from his every pore. Deep in thought, he tugged the white fringe of beard that fanned from his chin.

"I'd wager it's the flux," Hicks said. "They both shit themselves. You can surely smell that. I'd say by their ashen color they passed a good deal of blood when their bowels turned to water."

"Their berths would have been full of blood then," Bell said. "I barely saw any."

Hicks shrugged. "The storm last night gave us a soaking. Much water as we took on, it probably washed into the stinking stew on the hold floor."

Pearson contemplated this in silence. The look on his face told Bell he was unconvinced.

Hicks claimed he had served as a surgeon with Washington's army, but few in the crew gave much credence to his medical advice. He administered the same stinking yellow ointment for any external malady and watered brandy for everything else. Each of the ten slaves who'd taken ill on the previous voyage had shit themselves to death, along with two of the crew.

If he had any such qualifications, wisdom went, why would he suffer with the rest of them on a stench-laden slave ship?

"Whatever it is, Surgeon, it came on with speed and without warning," the skipper said. "We need to make sure it doesn't wipe out our entire cargo by the time we make Charleston."

"We should turn back to the coast and demand a new stock," Bevan said. "We're only a week out. You can put the fear of God

in that Dutch cunt. Threaten to tell the other American captains about him passing off sickly Negroes."

"We don't have the luxury," Pearson said. "That storm off the Bahamas cost us dearly in time in transit to the Gold Coast. If we want to make our bonus, including the slave you've been promised, we cannot afford another delay."

"Sod the bonus," Bevan said. "Doesn't make a difference if we're left without stock—or a crew. You heard about the *Dynamic*, didn't you? By the time it sailed into New Orleans, the flux had taken more than half its sailors and all but four slaves."

"I'm well aware of the *Dynamic*'s sorry fate, but we've reached the point of no return," the captain said. He cleared his throat, signaling the end of the debate. "We continue to South Carolina."

Pearson nudged the whip-wounded slave with his boot. The man's head turned to the side. His open eyes stared eerily in Bell's direction. They shone bright, showing none of the cloudiness he'd seen in the eyes of some of the dead slaves hauled topside on previous voyages.

"Any further sign of sickness in the hold, Mr. Hicks, tell me immediately," the captain said. "This cannot and will not spread."

"I suggest we bring them up daily for air and a constitutional," Hicks said. "But if that fails, they're still cramped too tight to quarantine. What brigs gain in speed, they lose in space."

Pearson examined the surgeon with cold eyes. "I asked a medical opinion, not advice on how to run a ship. I travel quickly, pick my stock judiciously and pack them light. Those incompetents who cram 150 Negroes into their slow-moving tubs often lose the majority before they sail into port."

"My apologies, sir," Hicks said. "But what if more take ill?"

"We pitch them over the side to stop the spread. We contain our losses. This is a business, after all."

* * *

After supper, the crew fetched the slaves from the hold. They shambled onto the deck, chained at wrist and waist, squinting against the blood-red light of the setting sun. Follett pumped water over them as they moved under the masts, prodded forward by a pair of sailors with long wooden poles.

The Africans shook the water from their shaved heads. Some quaked and shivered in the chilling air.

Bell dropped down, back against the railing. He pitied the bunch, wondering how many fully understood the fate that waited for them in America. He'd found his freedom, but none of them would likely be so lucky.

He cracked his copy of Homer's *Odyssey*, intent on making the best of the dying light. He'd read the book on his first voyage with Pearson. Its tales of gods and suitors and six-headed sea beasts diverted his mind from the brutality of his own dangerous voyage. He'd hoped it would do the same this time out.

Once more. Just one more passage.

With the sale of his share, he would be free of this life, positioned well enough to leave South Carolina and buy land in Philadelphia he could call his own.

When Alice had refused to leave Rembert Plantation with him, she told him they could never be safe, never be free, unless they owned land.

Curly-haired Thompson, the sailmaker, positioned himself below the mainmast and began sawing on his fiddle. Follett joined on a concertina so battered Bell wondered how it could even push air. The instruments drifted in and out of tune, and Bell was eventually unsure whether the pair even played the same song.

"Let's see some dancing, niggers," Bevan shouted over the racket.

He snapped his whip near the Africans' bare feet. A pair of sailors prodded them with shit hoes until they began swaying side to side in loose time to the music.

Bell had no sooner cracked the weathered leather cover of his book as Dowd tumbled down beside him, a tin mug clenched in his hand. The man's long hair fell in his face and his rum reek nearly matched that of Hicks the surgeon.

"Entertainment not to your liking?" Dowd asked. Bell watched the drunken sailor struggle to pry off a boot.

"Not the worst I'd heard, but certainly not a match for a decent book."

"The lad Thompson can play." Dowd nodded toward the sailmaker. "But that bag of shit Follett only seems capable of making racket. That concertina wheezes like our surgeon on a drunk."

"When isn't he on a drunk?" Bell asked. He turned his eyes back to his book, hoping Dowd wasn't too inebriated to take a hint.

"I can't say I blame him for imbibing." Dowd raised his mug. "Staying in a stupor is about the only way I can take life on this rotten piece of driftwood."

Bell closed the *Odyssey*, figuring it for a losing battle.

"I suppose it's preferable to debtor's prison," Dowd continued.

"At least in a jail cell, there's no chance of drowning."

The sailor laughed. "There's your sense of humor." He swallowed from his cup and winced against the burn. "This isn't your first time out, Bell. Tell me how a man can abide this life. Between the stench and the sickness and the way some in the crew have taken to arse-fucking the African women, you'd figure this place for the privies in a cheap whorehouse."

"I can abide it," Bell said. "Doesn't mean I like it." He raised an eyebrow. "And if someone's been having his way with the women below, he's risking Pearson's wrath. I've seen him flog men for that until their ribs showed."

Dowd swilled from his cup again. "Still, it seems odd to me that a freeman such as yourself would go on these voyages. Doesn't it bother you to lug your own countrymen back to America in chains?"

"First," Bell said, "they aren't my countrymen. I was born on American soil. My mother and father were from Barbados, sold to a plantation owner near Charleston."

"And second?"

"Second, I didn't put them in chains. They were captured before we got there, rounded up by rival tribes to trade for the guns and cloth we brought over. If they hadn't sold them to us, they would have sold them to the next ship that came along."

"Seems a callous view."

"I pity them." Bell shrugged. "But I can't help the way the world works. I became a freeman through my own tireless toil. Maybe some of them can do the same."

Thompson and Follett ended their song, and slipped into something that sounded vaguely like a hymn. One of Pearson's requests no doubt.

Bevan cracked his whip again, apparently disappointed at the slaves' languid attempt to dance. One screamed as the lash opened up his thigh.

Dowd shook his head. "As much as our skipper likes to quote the Good Book, you'd think he'd be more merciful to the poor bastards."

Bell said nothing.

He didn't like the way Pearson let thugs like Bevan and Follett indulge their cruelty on the Africans. Still, he'd worked for worse men. As he'd gained Pearson's respect, he'd earned the same treatment the man showed whites on his crew.

"So how'd you earn your freedom?" Dowd asked. "Biblical readings guilt your owner into becoming an abolitionist?"

"Not as such. He had no heir, so on his deathbed, he freed those of us he favored. I left with the clothes on my back and a bundle of his books."

Bell raised the *Odyssey*, noting that the light had dimmed enough that he now had no hope of getting in any reading. Dowd, while a drunk, wasn't the worst conversationalist on the *Lombard*.

"The ones he didn't favor?"

"Sold in auction," Bell said. "Trust me, I worked plenty hard to win his blessing. I took an interest in the master's books and he taught me to read, mostly it seemed so I could study the Bible."

"So what do you think of that book, Bell? You figure there's much truth to its talk of angels and devils?"

"Hard to know. I hear abolitionists quoting from the same Bible as the preachers who claim black folk deserve slavery because they're cursed by God."

Dowd issued a derisive snort. "I suppose the Book's got some interesting parables, but I don't hold much faith that either everlasting paradise or torment wait for us after death. Man makes his own heaven or hell. And this floating chamber pot is most definitely hell."

Bell didn't disagree.

* * *

The next morning, the crew discovered four more bodies, this time three women and the only child in the hold. Like the others, their flesh had gone pale gray, and once again, Hicks was at a loss to fully explain their demise.

Bell and the two others accompanied the doctor as he went through the hold, peering into the Africans' mouths and jamming a finger into their anuses. He dispensed medicine to each from a blue bottle Bell hadn't seen before. Bell doubted the potion was any more effective than the surgeon's stock of watered brandy.

"Mr. Bell, have you seen this damage to the hold?" Hicks asked after he slipped the blue bottle into his waistcoat. He nodded at a rotted plank high on the wall. The wood had peeled away, leaving a black hole no longer than a man's forearm and perhaps twice in height.

"New to me," Bell said, voice muffled by the neckerchief he held over his nose and mouth to blunt the smell. He had no idea whether the cloth could prevent contagion but it couldn't hurt.

He stood on tiptoes and peered at the opening. Truth was, he couldn't remember whether he'd noticed it before. The rotted plank was one of many on the deteriorating ship. On the passage over, Bell had crawled the hull sunrise to sundown, replacing warped and weathered timber.

"See it's fixed quickly," the surgeon said. "Stale air from the bilge could be filtering through the opening. Standing water carries many bad humors."

Bell wondered how any air could be more stale and vile than that in the slave hold. Even so, he nodded and fetched his tools.

* * *

Bell returned to the hold alone, neckerchief bound around his face.

He held his measuring string against the opening and realized the wood around it, while soft with the beginnings of decay, was far less rotten than any he'd replaced on the first leg of the voyage.

Long splinters splayed at the end of the broken plank. That suggested a blow from the other side had shattered the wood—a blow that would have come from between the hold wall and outside hull.

Bell dismissed the idea. There was no room between the two walls for anything but rats. He extended his hand into the dark hole. It sunk no deeper than his forearm before his palm struck hard wood.

Instead of being broken from the interior, it seemed more likely that someone in the crew—or worse, one of the slaves—had pried it away from the outside.

At that instant, Bell became keenly aware of the Africans' gaze. He turned and faced thirty-four sets of eyes staring from the berths' deep shadows. Those of the tall man with the scarred head smoldered with the most intensity.

* * *

"I warn you, Africans are a murderous race," Bevan said, tapping the mess table with a long finger to make his point. Several in the crew grumbled in agreement, Follett the loudest. "If one is getting loose, it's a matter of time before he frees the rest and we have a goddamned mutiny."

"The men checked the slaves' irons and they're secure," Captain Pearson said. "I'm confident of it, Mr. Bevan, and that should be reason for you to be as well."

"I swept through the hold to see if one is hiding something that could pick a lock," Bell said. "Nothing."

"And how do we know, Nigger George, that you actually checked them irons?" Follett asked. "Maybe you'd like to see your kind kill us whites in our sleep."

Dowd spoke up. "Don't be a fool. I saw him check."

Pearson held up a hand, calling for silence.

"I don't think any of us know what ripped away that plank. It's possible the damage has been there since we left America. Keep your eyes open and report to myself or Mr. Bevan if you see anything suspicious, but I'm confident none of the Africans is getting free."

He dismissed the crew.

Bell returned to the hold, masked again with his neckerchief. He scoured the walls for any more damage and found none.

Using the hook end of his hammer, he pried out the remnants of the damaged plank and slipped a new one in place, looking over his shoulder as he fitted it.

The slaves' eyes followed Bell the duration of his work. Their knuckles gripped the edges of their wooden shelves as if they feared sliding out of them onto the floor.

Their terse whispers reminded him of hissing snakes.

What do they know?

The crew had been thorough in their search of the hold. Still, Bell couldn't shake the tall, scarred African's dagger-sharp gaze. He imagined the man leading the rest of the freed captives across the deck in a silent and murderous prowl toward the crew's quarters.

Sleep evaded Bell that night. He turned over in his hammock, tense and dry mouthed. His eyes popped open at every creak from the timbers above.

* * *

The night passed without a mutiny, but just after dawn, cries in half a dozen dialects summoned Bell and the others to the slave hold.

The Africans screamed—some in panic, others in fury. They strained against their chains and grabbed at the crew. The sharp smell of fear threatened to overpower the reek of human waste.

A woman thrust her hand from the lower berth, seizing the hem of Bell's shirt. She pulled at the cloth and pleaded in a language he couldn't understand. Her eyes were wild with fright.

Bevan uncoiled his whip and ordered the Africans silent. When they ignored him, Follett grabbed a shit rake from the wall and jabbed its sullied end into the berths. The slaves recoiled, covering their heads with their hands.

Bell pulled away from the frightened woman, feeling his shirt rend in her tight grasp. He blundered backward into Thompson, who knelt by one of the lower shelves.

The sailmaker, face grim and drawn, held up a slave's limp, ashen arm.

More dead sprawled in the berth beside their comrade, cold, gray and immobile as lumps of unfired clay.

As Bell and the rest hoisted the six new corpses to the deck, a chilling realization settled in: a quarter of the *Lombard*'s human cargo had expired in three days' time.

* * *

When Bell slipped unnoticed from the mess, the rest of the crew were still pounding fists on tables and arguing whether the disease strictly preyed upon Africans or whether it could also spread to whites.

Pearson demanded an around-the-clock watch be stationed in the slave quarters, and Bevan argued that the entire stock be dragged to the deck for a flogging to frighten them from attempting mutiny.

Hicks, smelling especially fragrant of rum that morning, had postulated theories about poisonous phlegm in the Africans' lungs. He advocated a mass bleeding.

Bell had heard enough.

He descended the ladder into the slave hold, toting an armload of timber and his tool belt. He found the section of wall

he'd repaired the day before. The new board—several shades lighter than the wood around it—was easy to spot. It remained unmolested.

Bell propped his timber in a corner and continued the search, running his hands along the worn wood until he found a new breach, this time lower on the wall. It yawned from a dark corner between the water barrel and the bundled shit hoes. Talons of splintered wood splayed at its edges.

Like the previous, it was no wider than a single plank. And it too appeared to have been broken with a blow from the opposite side of the wall.

Bell knelt in front of the hole, careful to avoid a slick of excrement running from the lower berth. Shards of ruined wood littered the floor.

Frantic whispers sounded in the slave berths to Bell's rear. He looked over his shoulder and the whispers stopped.

The Africans watched him, their bodies tense enough to snap. As if they knew that by kneeling at the opening he had put himself in the worst sort of danger.

The tall, scarred man licked his lips. The look in his eyes no longer seemed penetrating and treacherous but panicked. He was scared—terrified of what lurked beyond the wall.

Bell lowered his face toward the black hole and a muscle twitched in his neck. A faint scratch sounded inside the wall. He pulled back, hair prickling on his arms and neck.

He waited for the scratching sound to come again but heard nothing.

The temperature in the hold seemed to plummet, as if the Africans' silence had chilled the room. Sliding the hammer from his belt, Bell again leaned toward the missing plank.

Something small and dark exploded from the blackness, flying toward Bell's face. He flopped backward, swinging wild with his hammer.

The slaves gasped as a chorus. Some shrieked.

Bell rolled over and rose to a crouch, hammer at the ready. A foot-long brown rat—large, but by *Lombard* standards, not

abnormal—scurried along the deck, dragging its balls and a bare pink tail.

It disappeared behind the water barrel.

Bell gulped in a deep breath and wiped sweat from his brow. He grabbed a new plank from his bundle of wood and secured it with four nails.

He couldn't finish the work quickly enough.

* * *

Bell descended into the cargo hold, now more unsure than ever of what had claimed the slaves' lives. He wondered whether the debate in the mess continued and what ludicrous theories Bevan, Hicks and the rest spewed.

Someone, or something, was ripping holes in the walls to gain access to the slave hold. He doubted anyone could maneuver in the narrow spaces between the walls and the hull. But that didn't rule out delivering some kind of disease or poison that way. Maybe someone had introduced a snake or poisonous insects into the walls.

Bell's lantern flickered over barrels of palm oil, bags of beans and crates of breadfruit. Shadows danced across the hold's high ceiling. The stink of the slave quarters above mingled with the odors of moldering fabric and rotting foodstuffs. It puzzled Bell why the *Lombard*'s living cargo was crammed into a hold too small to stand in, while dry goods earned extra headspace.

Something clattered at the far end of the hold, beyond the aura of his lantern. He figured it at first for a rat. Then a high human wail drifted from the narrow alley that zigzagged between piled boxes, barrels and sacks. Bell extinguished the lantern and reached for the hammer slung in his belt.

He moved through the darkness. The dank air became heavy and suffocating. The wailing voice broke the silence again and he recognized it as female. It cried out in anguish.

One of the slaves.

Rhythmic male grunts joined the woman's voice.

Bell tightened the grip on his hammer and navigated the aisle toward the source of the sounds. A faint light flickered from behind a tower of crates.

His foot creaked on a weak board and he stopped, wincing at the sound. The grunts from behind the crates ceased.

Bell's pulse pounded. He held his breath.

Two male voices, one low and coarse, the other higher and more refined, seemed to debate for a moment.

If a pair of crewmembers was molesting a slave, Bell was in his right to identify and report them. But he had no idea how the guilty parties would react. Possibly, given the quality of the men pulled into the slave trade, with fists and knives.

He readied his hammer. The handle felt slick in his hand, now wet with perspiration.

The debate stopped and the grunts resumed. So did the woman's piercing, gutted cries.

Danger be damned, he had to stop the rape. Or, failing that, at least tell Pearson who had committed it.

Bell held his breath and crept up to the stack of crates. He stepped light, fearing another complaint from the soft wood beneath his feet, and peered around the corner.

There, bathed in the light of a guttering candle, Bevan heaved over a female slave doubled over an oil barrel. His pants bunched loose at his ankles. Follett, by the looks of the tousled frizz of red hair, stood with his back to Bell, pinning the struggling slave's raised arms to the wall.

Bell weighed whether to stop the rape or retreat quietly and report it to Pearson. His stomach flipped as he realized his word might not stand against Bevan's.

The woman wriggled under Bevan, trying to throw him off, but the mate banged her head against the barrel. A hollow thud echoed through the hold.

"Wild little bitch, ain't she?" Bevan's red-bearded toady cackled, baring putrescent teeth. "Way she fights, ain't no way she's carrying the flux."

The woman kicked again. Bevan sidestepped the raised leg, pulling out of her. Follett brought his fist down on the back of the

woman's head and her face smashed into the hold. The smack reverberated in the closed space.

"*Stop!*" Bell stepped from his hiding place, fist clenched tight around the hammer. "Let her go!"

Bevan whirled, yanking up his pants. The look on his face, initially of panic, turned into one of rage. Follett flung the woman and she sprawled on her back. Blood slicked her teeth and lips.

"You don't give orders on this brig, Nigger George," Bevan said, tucking his cock back into his pants. "At least, not to me. Not to mention, it's goddamned rude to sneak up on a man during union."

Follett reached into his boot and a steel blade glinted in the dull yellow light.

"As first mate, I presume you know Captain Pearson's rules about the treatment of slaves," Bell said, readying his own weapon.

"So you fancy yourself a barrister now, do you, Bell?" Bevan smirked. "You may lug books around to show off, but I doubt that ape brain of yours understands a word of them."

Bevan grabbed for Bell's neckerchief and Follett, knife in hand, circled to his right. Bell whipped with his hammer, grazing the sailor's temple.

Follett choked out a pained gasp and hurled his considerable weight into Bell's torso. Bell tumbled backward, pinned to the hull.

Bevan twisted the hammer from his hand.

Bell squirmed to free himself but stopped after he felt the cool touch of Follett's dagger against his cheek.

"You'd best keep quiet about what you saw," Bevan said. His face hovered so close to Bell's that he could see the pores in his nose. His breath bore the biting stink of the ship's cheap rum. "You stick your nose into my business, Nigger George, and I'll have Follett here cut it off."

The oaf let out a wheezing laugh and the tip of his blade slipped deep into Bell's nostril. Its keen edge tugged at skin.

"I'd have me a tobacco pouch out of that ugly black thing," Follett said. His breath reeked worse than Bevan's.

The slave woman, now curled up next to the barrel, sobbed. She wiped blood from her mouth.

"You cut on me and Pearson will keelhaul the both of you. Be assured of that." Bell struggled to keep his voice steady. His throat constricted as he spoke. "You know what he thinks about sailors rutting on slaves they don't own."

"Don't own *yet*," Bevan said between clenched teeth. He jerked his head to the crying woman. "I've got one coming to me as my share, and that healthy filly there is the one I choose. Understood?"

Follett's blade twisted in Bell's nostril, as if scribing a question mark at the end of the word. Bell flinched and the knife tip punctured skin. Something warm and wet rolled down his lips.

"Understood?"

"Yes," Bell exhaled.

Bevan drove a fist into Bell's stomach. His accomplice stepped away and Bell tumbled to his hands and knees, gasping for breath.

"One word, Bell, so help me one, and Follett and I will find you in the middle of the night," the mate said. "We'll jab you up the ass with a broken shit hoe and throw you over the side. We can ask the sharks if free nigger tastes any better than slave nigger."

Bevan clapped Follett on the shoulder and the pair departed the hold, leaving Bell to clean up the woman and return her to her shackles and hard wooden berth.

* * *

Death skipped over the slave hold that night, the first after Pearson had ordered an armed watch posted. Instead, it visited the crew's quarters.

Bell awoke at dawn to a commotion at the other end of the narrow, claustrophobic dormitory. He slipped out of his hammock, still groggy and unsteady on his feet.

Dowd and Thompson shook a sailor named Guthrie, yelling in his ear. Bell and the rest circled around the unresponsive man.

He hung in his hammock like a dead fish in a net, mouth gaping and eyes open wide. The knuckles of one dangling hand scraped the floorboards. The sunrise through the porthole cast an unnatural orangey glow over his skin, gone white as china.

* * *

Guthrie's funeral preparations took place quickly. No one wanted to handle the body more than necessary. Hicks made his routine examination and Thompson hurriedly sewed it inside a length of canvas.

The service also ended in haste. None knew much about the man, who was on his first voyage with the *Lombard*. The majority of the event consisted of Pearson reading from his Bible and leading the crew in a recitation of the Lord's Prayer.

Afterward, the remaining crew gathered in the mess. Bell read the concern on their faces, especially those like Dowd who hadn't been out before.

A few gnawed at hard tack and breadfruit. Several sloshed rum into their tankards even though it wasn't yet noon.

"The flux appears to be running rampant through our human cargo and now it's made a jump to the crew," Hicks said. He leaned against the wall, seemingly for support. Bell wondered whether the man's girth and age caused him to be so unsteady or if his rum regimen had begun at dawn.

"That much is obvious, surgeon." Pearson shot Hicks a withering look. "The question is what we do to stop the spread to the rest of the crew." He seemed distant and distracted, as if calculating his escalating financial loss without aid of paper and quill.

"We must cut to cure," Hicks said. "We should examine the remaining slave stock and look for early signs of infection. Yellowing eyes, pus at the gums, blood in the rectum."

"There he goes again with the arseholes," Dowd whispered to Bell. "Worse than any buggerer."

"Those with early signs must go overboard," the surgeon said.

"Along with our profits," Pearson objected. "I'll remind you, part of your pay is based on what we deliver back to Charleston."

Mutters spread among the assembled men. Bell thought he heard someone suggest throwing the sawbones over the side.

Bevan raised a hand and stepped forward. "With all respect, Captain, the surgeon is correct. At the rate this disease is spreading, it could wipe out every one of us in a week."

"It'll end worse than the *Dynamic*." Follett slammed his tankard on the table. "The ship'll wash ashore with nothing but dead men aboard."

"Not only our profits but our lives are at stake," Bevan agreed. "The only answer is to hurl the sick ones overboard."

Bell wondered how much of Bevan's eagerness to drown the Africans was an effort to cover his and Follett's violation of the women. No telling how many they had dragged down to the cargo hold the week before the deaths.

"What makes us so sure this is the flux?" Dowd asked, looking around the room. He seemed surprisingly sober. "All of us have seen someone succumb to the disease, but I wager none has seen it work so fast."

"Nor leave dead men pale and bloodless," Bell agreed. "What if a man or an animal is sneaking below and taking their lives? I've found holes in the inner hull that someone or some*thing* might squeeze into and gain passage to other parts of the ship."

He looked at Bevan as he spoke.

"Absurd," Bevan croaked, shaking his head. "No man or animal could drain a body of blood and without leaving so much as a single mark. Let's end this discussion and throw the sickly blacks over the side. Sink the lot of them for all I care."

"Enough." The captain held up a hand to silence his officer. "Continue, Mr. Bell."

"I don't know how this stowaway is draining their blood, but Hicks has also seen one of the breaches," Bell said.

"What I saw even a small child would have a hard time squeezing through," Hicks slurred. "Mr. Bell, spook stories may provide fine entertainment on the plantation, but they have no place in a serious medical discussion."

"Stop wasting our time, nigger," Follett grumbled. He gulped from his mug.

Pearson cleared his throat. "I'm unconvinced we have a stowaway animal or murderer in our midst, but I'm also not convinced that dumping our cargo is the only recourse." He turned to Hicks. "Surgeon, increase your dose of medicine for the remaining slaves. Double it, if you can."

Pearson walked to the door. "The rest of you, get back to your duties."

Bell rose, ready to resume his aborted search below deck. Something was awry, and Bevan was either too stupid to sense it or, worse, eager to cover it up.

"You speak well." The mate stepped into his path, practically bumping the brass buttons of his coat against Bell's chest. The cords in Bevan's neck stood out taut over his collar. His face was red as a blistering sunburn. "Just mind you don't end up saying the wrong thing."

He tweaked Bell's nose, still tender from the nick by Follett's knife.

Bell stepped back. "Why'd you take such offense to my point? The skipper thought it worth hearing. Are you trying to make sure the women go over the side to keep your and Follett's secret?"

"No matter how much you think Pearson respects you, my word is bond against a black's," Bevan said, smirking. "I'll see that he nails your tongue to the mainmast and chains you in the hold with the rest of the animals."

Bevan turned on his heel.

Bell shook with anger. He closed a fist, fighting the urge to lay the man flat. Instead, he watched the mess door slam behind him.

"That fucking bastard is the first who should be thrown off the boat," Dowd said. He leaned in the kitchen doorway, a rum bottle dangling between two fingers.

Bell nodded, not in the mood to indulge Dowd's complaining. He headed for the door, but Dowd grabbed his arm.

"Why are you here, George? I'm here because I have no choice, but it doesn't seem like you're one step away from the jailors."

Bell stiffened. His ears and face flushed. He fought the urge to turn his anger on Dowd.

"You think I have other choices?" he asked. "When I left the plantation, it's not like I was really a free man. It's not like I could ride into Charleston, hang a shingle and work as a carpenter. That's not what being a free black means. It means I could slop shit and take whatever abuse the whites sent my way."

"I'm sorry."

"I suppose you can't understand what it's like to be seen as inferior no matter how hard you work, no matter how much you read and think."

"Maybe I'd like to understand. How'd you get here, Bell?"

Bell breathed deep. Beyond the façade of drunken buffoonery, Dowd wasn't an abusive lout like Bevan or Follett. In fact, today—when it mattered—he'd been an ally, perhaps the closest thing he had on the *Lombard* to a friend.

At the least, he owed the man civility.

"When I left the plantation, I ended up in a little settlement called Rabbit Bend," Bell said. "First place I could find work. It was a settlement built by whites that trade with the sugar plantations. The biggest, Rembert Plantation, must have had three hundred slaves. I labored for a white carpenter whose consumption of ale began at sunup. He paid me pennies to finish work he was too drunk to complete. Eventually, he rented me the apartment behind his shop."

"Seems a far better place than the *Lombard*."

"It was. I thought so at the time, anyway." Bell paused. "That is, until I met Alice Dryden." The name was strange to say. Despite the pain it bore, it still somehow felt good on his lips.

"Alice, eh?" Dowd smiled, raising an eyebrow. "So romance enters the plot. Sit a while and tell me about lovely Alice, and don't spare a single detail." He gestured toward the mess table.

Bell laughed. It was difficult to stay mad around Dowd. Realizing the man wouldn't let him go without elaborating, he

slid a bench out from the table and sat. Dowd slumped down opposite him.

"Alice was a woman from the plantation, a slave," Bell said. "Most beautiful woman I'd ever seen. She was proud, almost regal. Skin so smooth and delicate, it begged to be touched. Her clothes were finer than many I'd seen on white women."

A tightness spread through his chest, a sudden worry he was speaking too freely. He paused, realizing this was the first time he'd mentioned Alice to anyone on the *Lombard*. He'd always been spare on details of his life, fearing the whites in the crew would seize on them, add them to their arsenal of torments.

"I want to hear about more than her clothes, good man." Dowd smiled. "Tell me how you met this lovely Alice."

"I first saw her when I was cutting wood outside the shop. She rode into town in a wagon next to another house slave, an older man dressed in a fine suit. I watched them ride by and couldn't help but stare. She looked down at me, didn't smile, but I could see something in her eyes. Something that told me she liked what she saw—even though my own threadbare clothes were grimy with sweat and sawdust."

The memory of that gripped Bell, vivid as if it had been yesterday. The mahogany-skinned beauty in the maroon dress and crisp white bonnet had no reason to acknowledge him, none to give him a second glance. Yet her bright eyes had locked with his for the few heartbeats it took the wagon to bounce past. They seemed to acknowledge his worth as a man, as a human being.

"Please tell me you chased this stunning beauty," Dowd said. "Not much of a story if you didn't."

"Trust me, I didn't have a choice. After that look, I couldn't think of anything else. I asked around, found out she and the old man, a fellow named Louis Carlisle, rode into town every Wednesday and bought supplies for the Remberts. She'd shop for cloth and food. Him for hardware, tools and the rest. I found ways to run into her on the street, comment on the weather or the color of her dress. Eventually, I mustered up the courage for a joke. And, at that, she smiled at me. A dainty, shy smile that showed off

teeth like pearls. A few more 'chance meetings' and to my surprise, we were slipping off into my little room."

"And now we arrive at the good bit."

That *had* been the good bit, hadn't it? Those stolen meetings when he thought he'd found true love, someone to sustain him as he made his way in an unjust, uncaring world.

Bell remembered their first encounter in his cluttered shack—Alice's smooth hand on his cheek, the smell of rosewater on her neck as he pulled her close. He'd wondered then how a slave, even a trusted house slave, had access to such an intoxicating luxury.

"That scant hour we met every week became all I looked forward to," Bell continued. "It gave my pitiful work purpose. Especially when I found out Alice could read. We found solace in books. Talked about what we'd read, what they meant. We debated them. She even sneaked a few from the Remberts' house for me."

Dowd's face sagged. "You disappoint me, Bell. Surely you did more than sit around with your noses in books."

"Are you always so inquisitive?"

"My life in taverns made me a good listener to others' troubles." Dowd shrugged. "I can't imagine Alice's master was happy with your… erm, forwardness."

"Robert Rembert didn't know. But, sadly, old Louis Carlisle did. I always met Alice when he was busy with his buying excursions, but I discovered later he'd somehow pieced it all together. But, that's not important until later. Around the time Alice and I were sneaking off, I happened upon a newspaper and read about Pennsylvania's abolition act, about how the Quakers there would harbor runaway slaves. I realized that not every place was like South Carolina, that if I could buy a horse and ride Alice and myself north fast enough, we could find freedom."

Dowd swigged from the rum. "And that clearly didn't happen."

"No, it didn't. I saved my earnings, did without food some days, so I could buy an old nag. One day, while we lay curled up on my pallet, I told Alice my plan. About how the Society of

Friends could see we got safe harbor. I expected her to show me that bright smile and ask how soon we could ride away."

"And did you?"

"We didn't." Bell winced. The words stung to speak aloud. "Alice told me she wouldn't leave. She said as long as I had no money and no property, I was no better than a slave myself. It crushed me. I just sat silent and watched as she slipped back into her dress and bonnet and stole out my door."

The smell of rosewater, he recalled, hung in his room for days after her departure, a bittersweet reminder of his loss.

"Did you see her again?" Dowd asked.

"No. The following week, another woman came with Carlisle in her place. I wrote a letter to Alice, begging her to see me one last time. I hoped that if I explained myself and gave the letter to Carlisle, she would agree to ride away with me."

"Good God, man." Dowd whistled and raised his bottle in salute. "I'm not sure whether to toast your bravery or stupidity."

"In retrospection, it was solely the latter. Carlisle laughed when I gave it to him. I had been too much a naïf to understand Alice was Robert Rembert's favorite for a reason. He told me people in the town joked openly about pale-skinned slave children on the plantation that had his mouth and eyes. He told me he'd seen her slip away with me."

The phantom smell of rosewater tickled Bell's nostrils. It was during that conversation with Carlisle that he'd finally understood who had gifted it to Alice. Now, the dense sweetness just reminded him that rose petals fade, drop and rot, just as their brief time together had.

Dowd said nothing but passed the rum. Bell took a long swallow of the bottle's sweet, burning contents and continued.

"The next night, three of Rembert's drivers dragged me out of my room and beat me half to death while the constable and my employer looked on. They rode me well out of town, dumped me and told me that if I returned, Rembert would have my head on a pike."

He drank again and slid the rum back to Dowd. He wondered if he should feel some relief finally telling the story to someone. Somehow, he hadn't.

"I lay there, wishing I could die. When I didn't, I dragged myself up, face so swollen I could barely see, and stumbled away from the Lowlands. After a few days, I made my way to Charleston. I'd read that sailors made good wages, and it seemed like a way to put myself far from South Carolina while I saved money for Pennsylvania." He shook his head. "But the merchant captains didn't want a black man with no sea legs and I fell in with Pearson's sad crew."

"Sad we are, aren't we?" Dowd said. "So do you think Alice sanctioned the beating? Or did Carlisle even tell her about the letter?"

"I don't know." Bell stood. Too often, he'd wondered the same thing, and talking about it any longer with Dowd certainly wouldn't lead him to an answer. "All I know is the two of us have work to do. And I'd like to finish it while there's still reading light left."

* * *

Bell's sleep came in restless fits. He'd hoped to dream of Odysseus turning his vengeful bow on Penelope's suitors. Instead, he was stalked by memories of the Rembert's bully boys and their rain of pummeling fists.

The next morning, he went about his topside duties tired and groggy. He lent his back to the ropes while Thompson and four others hoisted a newly repaired topgallant sail into place.

He watched Thompson scale the mast's rope shrouding, wondering where Dowd had gone. He had a noticeable talent for avoiding hard labor.

A hand clapped his shoulder, and the sailor made his well-timed appearance.

"While you were busying yourself with this ache-inducing labor, I made a discovery of my own below deck," Dowd whispered. "I think you'll want to see it."

Bell followed Dowd into the cargo hold, curious what the man had in mind. They stopped below a tumble of overstuffed sacks that rose almost to the ceiling. Flour streamed from a rupture in the bottom sack. Black balls of rat shit dotted the floor.

"Tell me you didn't drag me down here to show me rats have been in the flour," Bell said. "Anyone unfortunate enough to have eaten one of the cook's biscuits knows that much."

"No, up there, where the hull joins the deck above us."

Dowd raised the lantern and light flickered across the sloping hold. Darkness showed through a narrow space where yet another plank had been sheared away. The opening grinned two feet long but no wider than Bell's hand.

"We're just below the holes you found in the slave deck, aren't we?" Dowd asked.

The sailor was right.

"And the crawlspace," Bell said.

"Crawlspace?" Dowd rocked his head, puzzled.

"This ship ran rum before it hauled slaves. There's a false floor in the closet of the crew's quarters, leads to a hidden floor between the slave hold and this one. It's so narrow a man could barely crouch inside, but someone could certainly wriggle through."

Bell found a foothold in the pile of flour sacks and clambered up. "Hold the lantern high," he called over his shoulder. Once he reached the top, he grabbed a ceiling strut to steady himself.

Jagged shards of wood jutted dagger-like from one end of the new opening. The plank had been snapped in half, just like the other holes he'd found.

Bell ran a hand below the breach. His fingers found deep grooves in the wood.

"Bring up the light," he called.

The bags rocked and he reached down a hand to steady Dowd as he climbed. The lantern shook on his way up. Shadows writhed around them.

Dowd made it to the top and focused the lantern's bull's-eye on the opening. Four deep gashes marred the plank below, each an inch deep and four times as long.

The marks' shape and spacing left little doubt what had left them.

"Some kind of claw," Dowd said. He screwed up his face as if he doubted what he saw.

Hair prickled on the back of Bell's neck as it occurred to him that whatever had torn the wood away could lurk just beyond the wall. The space was too small to fit a human but that didn't rule out something just as dangerous.

"An ape? A cat?" Dowd slid the knife from his belt scabbard, apparently recognizing the same thing.

Bell shrugged, wishing he'd brought his hammer.

Keeping a careful distance, he lowered his head. He held his breath and peeked into the hole.

Nothing launched itself at him this time.

Inside, more deep gashes scarred the wood of the exterior hull. He motioned for the lantern and Dowd moved it closer. The jaundiced light revealed more claw-like gashes as well as deeper, wider indentions in the wood. The larger ones looked as if someone had dug a hatchet into the planks.

Dowd leaned in for a better look. The bags shifted beneath them as if the entire pile might capsize. Dowd let out a yelp.

Bell's stomach pitched and he clutched the ceiling beam again for support.

"Careful," he said between clenched teeth. "You'll bring the whole pile down and snap both our necks."

Dowd steadied himself and craned his neck.

"Something's carved that wood all to hell," he said, squinting. "Surely we'd know if there was an animal on the ship."

"Unless it knew enough to keep itself hidden."

"One cunning beast," Dowd said.

* * *

Bell shook the scarred African's massive shoulder, and the man stirred in his narrow berth.

Dowd watched nervously from a spot near the ladder. He'd swapped out watch shifts with Follett so he and Bell could gain access to the hold.

The tribesman raised his head, blinking his eyes against the lantern light.

The older man lying next to him shrunk back, apparently anticipating the strike of a whip or shit hoe. Bristles of silver showed at the man's chin and temples.

"I know you can speak English," Bell said. "The men at the fort told me."

The big man's eyes burned with distrust. He scowled.

"What's your name?" he asked. "Mine is George Bell."

Dowd smiled uneasily and tapped his chest. "They call me Benjamin," he said. "Ben."

Bell motioned silence, wishing Dowd would keep quiet and watch the ladder for Follett and Bevan.

"Why do you want my name?" the African asked. "The men at the fort tell me you will only take it and give me a new one."

"Tell me your name and I will see that you keep it," Bell said.

The tribesman shook his head, apparently unimpressed with Bell's lying ability. "Kwame," he said, mouth wrenched into something between a smirk and a snarl. "You will not live long enough to see that I keep it."

Bell exhaled, discouraged. If simply dragging a name out of the man had been this difficult, he didn't have high hopes for the rest of the conversation.

"I know you've seen the thing that killed ten people in this hold," he said. "What is it?"

"Ask the whites you serve," Kwame said. "Ask these soulless ones why a demon haunts their ship. Their evil brought this curse on all of us."

"Is it an animal?" Bell asked. "Help me so we can find this thing and destroy it."

"I told you what it is."

"I don't believe in demons," Bell said. "Is it some kind of beast? A cat?"

Kwame laughed. "Men can kill a cat. This thing you cannot kill, not even with your guns, your steel and your whips."

The old man beside Kwame spoke. His voice had a high, melodic cadence. He motioned with a hand and his heavy chains banged against the berth.

Kwame listened as the man spoke, nodding in apparent agreement.

"This man is a *griot*," Kwame said when the man finished. "Do you know the *griots*? Wise men who sing and tell stories. He says he knows of the thing that haunts your ship. It's something so evil he refuses to say its name because even its name is a curse."

Kwame paused. He glared at Bell.

"I am not afraid to say its name because there is no worse curse than what I bear now." He raised his chained fists, making sure Bell got a good look at the thick manacles clamped around his wrists. "It is an *asanbosam*. You have been gone from our shores too long to know this word, George Bell, but now you will fear it."

"Tell me what this creature is so we can kill it," Bell said. "I'm trying to save all of you. Surely you understand that."

Dowd left his post by the ladder. He stood shoulder to shoulder with Bell. Nervous sweat dripped from his brow. His palm rested on the knife at his belt.

The *griot* spoke again. His speech bounced with an alluring rhythm. A sad wisdom showed in the man's eyes.

"He says the demon is draining the blood from our bodies first," Kwame translated. "And when we're gone, it will do the same to you and then to the whites."

"It's already started on the whites," Dowd said.

"It takes men when they sleep," Kwame said. "Once we knew that an *asanbosam* and not disease cursed this ship, we stopped sleeping. But it can kill men even when they don't sleep. It can hide in the cracks of tree trunks or swing down from their branches. It tears men's throats with teeth like iron. Its claws rip out their hearts."

Bell's stomach seized. He thought of the splintered wood, the deep claw marks below deck.

"You found the holes it made," Kwame said. "But you did not see the other marks it left with its feet." He pointed upward.

Bell swung the lantern around the hold. Deep hatchet-like gashes marked the ceiling, as if the thing had hung from the wood there as it closed in on the sleeping Africans.

Dowd's jaw flopped open. "Christ save us," he said.

Kwame shook his head. "Your god cannot save us. The more blood the *asanbosam* takes, the stronger it becomes."

"With your help—" Bell began.

"I cannot help unless I am free." Kwame motioned around the hold with a huge hand. "Unless *all* of us are free."

"I can't do that," Bell said. "If I release you, the white men will cut all of us down. Tell me how to find the *asanbosam* and kill it. You will be slaves in America. There's nothing I can do to stop that. But at least you will live."

"Slavery is not living," Kwame said.

"I was a slave, but I earned my freedom. You may be able to do the same."

The *griot* spoke again, gesturing at Bell with a scolding finger.

Kwame waited until the man finished and translated slowly, emphasizing each word. "He said you have not earned your freedom if you help the whites destroy your own kind. You have only earned the curse of the demon that stalks us."

* * *

A desperate chorus of screams penetrated the cargo hold while Bell replaced the broken plank. He dropped his hammer and scrambled down the heap of grain sacks, Dowd following just behind.

Halfway up the ladder, Bell recognized the voices as the Africans'. He hauled himself onto the deck and felt his soul slip away.

Follett and the rest of the sailors bound a dozen slaves wrist-to-ankle, forming a chain of humanity. Among them, Bell

recognized the *griot* and the woman Bevan had violated in the cargo hold. The sailors met their struggles and pleas with kicks and punches.

One of the women clawed at Follett's face and he drove a meaty fist into her stomach. Another sailor cracked the *griot* over the back with a thick wooden dowel. He screamed, collapsing to the deck.

Bevan paced a circle around the grisly work clenching a saber.

The skipper and surgeon stood aloof, arms folded. They watched the preparations dispassionately as if the crew was swabbing the deck or sewing sails.

"Captain, sir," Bell began. His voice quavered. "I thought you decided not to purge the holds."

"While you and Mr. Dowd were off doing God knows what, we found another of the crew dead," Pearson said. He didn't break his gaze from the sickening brawl. "Boatswain Dougherty succumbed this morning. We found him sprawled across the kitchen floor."

"Were there marks on his body?" Bell asked.

"Not a one," Hicks said. Liquor burned on his breath. "He seemed hale enough at sunrise and now his body is drawn and bloodless as the rest. I've never seen the likes of this plague."

"Which is exactly why any Negro showing signs of sickness is going overboard," Pearson said. "God rest their souls."

One of the African men wriggled on the deck, struggling to throw off his ropes. Follett kicked him in the midsection. Cursing, Bevan brought the hilt of his saber down on the groaning man's crown.

Dowd winced and turned his head.

"Please, sir—" Bell began.

Pearson raised a silencing hand.

"Enough. I know this will cut into our profits and leave you without a share, but the safety of my crew is paramount."

A cold, clammy sickness inched through Bell's body. He held silent, weighing what objection, if any, could change Pearson's mind.

Dowd pointed to the slaves. "Surely the struggle of these men and women show they're not ill."

"Sir, Dowd and I don't think these deaths are the result of disease but something stalking the ship," Bell said. "The Africans think a creature, a wild animal of some sort, found its way onboard."

Hicks puffed his jowls. "Absurd. The superstitious workings of primitive minds."

"It's decided, Bell," Pearson said. "Either carry on with your duties or help us get these diseased wretches over the side."

Two crewmen rolled a cracked millstone into place beside the slaves. Follett threaded the rope joining the Africans through its central hole. He knotted it in place.

Seeing this, the African who Bevan had struck down, awkwardly scrambled to his feet. Blood poured from a wide gash at his hairline.

The man hurled himself at Follett, bringing his bound hands down on the sailor's back.

Bevan skewered the African through the stomach with his saber. The man crumpled, screaming. His hands grasped at the wound and blood pumped through his fingers.

Pearson's face tightened in irritation. "Enough! Get them over the side. *Quickly*."

Follett rose unsteady. Bevan joined him and the pair rolled the stone toward the pitching ocean. The rest of the men prodded the Africans toward the side, jabbing with icebreakers and pummeling with fists.

Bile burned in Bell's throat. He tried in vain to blot the doomed slaves' cries.

Bevan cut the dying African from the grim procession. He hoisted the man to his feet. Blood slopped across the deck as the mate dragged him to the side.

"This bastard doesn't deserve to sink quickly," Bevan called out. He kicked the slave's legs away, tumbling him into the ocean. The choppy waves below slashed like sharp blue blades.

The bound slaves kicked and hit back. Follett tried to roll the stone past them, but a pair of women clambered in front. Bell

couldn't tell whether they cursed or begged the sailors–perhaps both.

Bevan leaned against the rail, laughing and pointing downward. The bleeding man bobbed among the white tufts of sea foam, struggling to keep himself afloat with one hand. A trio of gray fins skimmed the surface in a wide circle around him.

Two other sailors joined Follett. They shoved the pleading women to the deck and kicked them into submission. Follett resumed rolling the millstone and heaved it into the sea. A tangle of black limbs followed the plummeting weight. The Africans flailed and clawed at the planks but disappeared over the side, one after the other.

Bell, weak and nauseated, leaned on the rail. His legs threatened to buckle. Beside him, Bevan unleashed a high-pitched cackle.

One of the fins circling the wounded African submerged. Seconds later, something jerked him beneath the waves and a billow of red appeared in his place.

"Serves the bastard." Bevan straightened himself and placed his hands on his hips.

Dowd turned away, steadying himself against the rail. The color drained from his face as if he'd seen an apparition. He dropped to his hands and knees, long hair falling around his face, and vomited across the deck.

The upper half of the African's body bobbed on the foam, its trunk trailing long shreds of skin. Another fin cut through the waves toward it.

Bell's stomach pitched with the movement of the ship. Bevan's hand clapped down on his shoulder.

"You blacks may smell awful, but apparently you don't taste bad," he said. The bootlick Follett, who had now wandered to the side, guffawed, exposing the blackened nubs of his few remaining teeth.

Bell whirled and punched Bevan in the mouth. The mate's legs buckled and he toppled backward onto the deck. Bell readied another punch, but Follett and the others fell on him fast. They held his arms and forced him to his knees.

Dowd took a tentative step toward the scrum but backed away. Sick pasted his shirt to his chest.

Bevan climbed to his feet, teeth bared like a rabid dog. He slid his saber from its scabbard.

"I'll cut your black heart out for that," he snarled. He rested the tip of his blade against Bell's breastbone. The chill point dug into his flesh.

Bell knew he should feel fear, but something else, a calm like sailing into the eye of a particularly vicious storm came over him.

"Cut me open then," he said. "My heart's no more black than yours."

"Stand down, Mr. Bevan!" Pearson shouted. "I administer discipline on this ship." He stepped into view beside his first mate and wrested the saber from his grip.

"The nigger struck me," Bevan protested. "He raised a hand to an officer."

"Exodus 21:20, Mr. Bevan." Pearson examined the gleaming edge of the saber as he spoke. "When a man strikes his male or female slave with a rod so hard that the slave dies under his hand, he shall be punished. If, however, the slave survives for a day or two, he is not to be punished, since the slave is his own property."

The captain raised the weapon and Bell met his eyes, determined not to flinch.

The blunt pommel came down on his head and his world became darkness.

* * *

A drenching of frigid seawater jolted Bell awake. He stirred, opening his eyes, now stinging with brine.

Bevan stood over him holding a bucket.

Bell's head throbbed. He tried to rise from the soaked deck but couldn't muster the strength.

The mate yanked him up by his collar and dragged him toward the fore of the ship. "Reckoning time is at hand, Nigger George. I'm sure Captain Pearson will have some choice verses for you on crime and punishment."

Dizzy, Bell stumbled to keep up. His legs felt distant and disconnected, as if he walked underwater. He shook his head, hoping to bring the world into focus. The foremast loomed ahead. Follett stood beside it, uncoiling a length of rope.

Pearson joined them below the fluttering sails. The sun seemed bone white against the cloudless sky.

"Bell, I thought you'd managed to overcome the wild instincts of your race," the captain said. "Sadly, your actions today betray your inability to do so. 'Cursed be Canaan. Let him become the lowest slave to his brothers.'"

Bevan thrust Bell's face into the mast and Follett wound a rope around his right wrist.

"I served you as well as any of these men," Bell said. "Better than some."

He spat in Follett's face.

A slap thundered in his ear and he dropped to his knees. Bevan dragged him to his feet again. Follett wiped viscous mucous from his red beard and yanked the rope. It bit into Bell's wrist.

"I will have discipline kept on this ship," Pearson said. "For striking an officer, you hereby relinquish your claim on your bonus, and you will receive no fewer than twenty lashes at the foremast at my own hands. As a reminder as to whence you've come and where you could end up again, you will spend the rest of this voyage in chains with the rest of your kind."

"God damn you," Bell shouted. "I'm a freeman recognized under law. Save your lashes for rapists and murderers like Bevan."

"On the *Lombard*, the only law that matters is my law," Pearson said. "I have no illusion that this is honorable work, but I do expect to lead honorable men."

Follett hoisted Bell's hands over his head and lashed them to the pegs jutting from the mast.

"A fitting punishment," Bevan said, checking the ropes. He yanked at one and it cut deeper into Bell's skin. "My only regret is I can't administer the flogging myself."

Bell looked over his shoulder.

Pearson, now stripped of his jacket, rolled up his sleeves. The rest of the crew stood behind him in a semicircle. Dowd looked down at his own feet.

The captain uncoiled his whip.

"Much is required from those to whom much is given, and much more is required from those to whom much more is given. Luke 12:48."

The first strike felt as if hot coals rained down Bell's back, the second as if someone had dug a dagger into the scorched flesh.

He blacked out some time after the tenth.

* * *

Bell awoke to a tickling around his mouth. Something fluttered over his lips as he lay on his side in the stinking slave berth. His back screamed in agony and his mouth tasted like he'd eaten mud.

He tried to wipe his mouth with the back of his hand. The chain from his manacle rattled against wood and he realized he could lift it little higher than his chest.

The tickling continued and Bell strained to open his crusted eyes. A white rat almost a foot long came into hazy view in front of him. It brazenly licked at spittle on his lips.

Bell jerked back his head and the rodent scurried away into the darkness, whipping a hairless tail as thick as a finger. He spat over the side of the rough wooden shelf and cursed.

Flies and dust swam in the single shaft of sunlight that streamed from the open hatch above. It illuminated the hold just enough for Bell to see the Africans on the other side of the aisle propped on their elbows, staring into his berth.

They narrowed their eyes in anger and muttered among themselves. Some pointed at the new arrival. Kwame, shaking his head, met Bell's gaze. He was unsure whether to read the African's look as derision or pity.

The captor had become the captive. Perhaps he'd been one all along. He'd been a fool to think Pearson or any of the others

respected him. That his service on this miserable ship would help him buy a safe haven in Pennsylvania.

There was, he thought to himself, no such thing as a free black man.

The slave next to him stirred. The man groaned and something spattered behind him. The smell of evacuated bowels, already dense in the stifling hold, became stronger. Bell turned his head and coughed.

He faded in and out of consciousness, a half sleep punctuated by the rocking of the ship, the occasional cries of his fellow captives and stinging pain in his back when each time he moved.

He couldn't sleep on his bloodied back, but resting face down brought its own discomfort. His ribs pressed against the hard wood and it put pressure on his bladder. Eventually, he had no choice but to urinate in his bunk. The warm fluid burned against his bare thighs.

The dusty shaft of sunlight eventually dimmed to dull gray and the hold eventually filled with stifling, impenetrable darkness. Bell was vaguely aware of another sailor descending the creaking ladder to take watch.

When he found sleep, he dreamed of the sugar plantation, of the green and sweeping cane fields. He heard screams as the master's drivers trained their whips on the field niggers. Briefly, he dreamed of Alice Dryden lying nude next to him, her bare breasts warm against his side.

"I can't go, George," she breathed into his ear. "I can't leave this place."

Several times Bell awoke to find the rat, or at least others that looked like it, sniffing at his lips and staring at him with black buckshot eyes.

* * *

In the morning, sailors clunked down the ladders, banging their buckets and slopping kankey into their captives' outstretched hands. As they worked their way up the aisles, Bell realized Hicks and Bevan were among them.

The man next to Bell struggled to raise himself on an elbow and Follett slopped a pile of the runny gruel onto the planks in front of him. The man dipped his fingers into it and raised them to his mouth. He looked disdainfully at Bell.

"Making new friends, are you, Nigger George?" Follett grinned down. "Better eat. You got a long journey ahead."

He plunged the ladle into the slop bucket with a nauseating splat. The sound reminded Bell of the man next to him shitting the berth. He realized that soon enough he would face the same indignity.

As much as Bell wanted to spit in Follett's face and refuse the kankey, he couldn't. His stomach groaned, empty for too long. His body needed food to repair itself.

He extended his left hand, licking his lips. Saliva filled his mouth as the sweet smell of the corn and palm oil momentarily cut through the hold's stink of shit, piss and sweat.

Follett lifted the ladle, but Bevan loomed over his shoulder and held his arm. Bell's stomach burned.

"Look at our proud freeman begging for his rations," Bevan said. "The law may be on your side on dry land, but at sea, a whole different set of rules prevail."

Bell said nothing.

"Don't worry," Bevan said. "You'll get slopped like the rest of these filthy hogs. I just want the surgeon to look at your back. I'd hate to see you succumb to your wounds and miss the pleasure of mingling with the rest of the savages."

Bevan grabbed Hicks by his upper arm and the surgeon staggered forward. His thinning white hair hung loose, two long strands dangling in his face like catfish whiskers. He slipped his salve bottle from his waistcoat and leaned into the bunk.

Bell clenched his teeth as the stinging salve touched his raw wounds. The rum reek of the doctor's breath and yellowed shirt was a welcome respite from the odor of human excrement.

When Hicks was done, Bell rested his head against the berth and drifted into unconsciousness.

This time, he dreamed that he walked amid tall yellowing grass toward the shade of a large, dark tree with branches draped

almost to the ground. A shadowy form moved among the rustling leaves, lurking just out of view.

* * *

An apocalyptically loud crack bolted Bell awake. Disoriented, he raised his head.

A second later, after a flicker of cobalt light illuminated the hold, he recognized the sound as thunder. The ship pitched and he slid against the man next to him. The shackles tugged at his wrists.

Whispers and cries sounded around him and the thunder reverberated through the ship. In the ghostly light that followed, Bell made out frightened faces peering from the rain-slicked berths.

The ship bounced as if boiling in a soup pot. Waves skittered over the deck and gushed into the hold. Cold, salty water sloshed over his naked body.

The sailor on guard dragged himself up the ladder, evacuating his drenched post. Shadow obscured the man's face, but Bell thought he saw Pearson's mop of curly hair.

A thunk resonated from the other end of the compartment, a sound too dull to be a distant clap of thunder. It repeated and Bell though it might be the loose hatch banging the hull.

Until he heard it a third time.

The sound wasn't deep and resonant enough to be coming from outside. It came from somewhere within the slave hold and Bell realized it was moving closer.

Thunk. Again. *Thunk*.

He slunk deep into the berth. His back burned as he drew away from the edge of his wooden shelf.

The sound repeated and he placed it somewhere above. His mind fixed on the image of the deep, hatchet-like incisions Kwame had pointed out.

A scream sounded to his left, then another. Chains rattled against wood and the hold became a cacophony of terror. Bell's

eyes darted through the darkness, trying to fix on what menaced his fellow captives.

Thunder rumbled again, but the flash that followed was short. Something moved against the timbers overhead, but Bell couldn't fix on it with any certainty.

The darkness returned and he resisted the urge to join the screamers. He heard the hatchet-like sound again.

Thunk. Thunk.

Bell's heart pounded. He shivered as if an icy breeze blew through the hold.

The noise stopped and Bell sensed something in the darkness in front of him. He couldn't see it, couldn't hear it, but he felt its presence. The man beside him recoiled, rattling his manacles.

Lightning flashed, and there, just outside his berth, hung the demon Kwame had described.

Even in the bright burst of lightning, the thing seemed amorphous, as if it absorbed light the way a sponge did water. Its skin seemed to take on the color of the stained wood around it.

The creature hung bat-like from the ceiling, dangling from backward-bending lower appendages that terminated not in feet but sharp, curving hooks.

Bell recoiled as the monstrosity's broad skull hinged open. It hissed, baring a thicket of iron-gray needles. The creature raised a long, sinewy arm, exposing rake-like talons the same color as its teeth.

Darkness flooded the hull again and the thing rushed into Bell's berth. He rolled to the side and felt the creature's bulk whisk by. Its warmth seemed to fill the space. The man beside him thrashed, limbs flailing against the wood.

Bell's scream was lost in the next explosion of thunder. He kicked and felt his foot connect with warm flesh, unsure whether it belonged to man or beast.

Chains banged against the walls and the screams intensified. Frantic, Bell joined the banging and screamed himself hoarse. Enough noise could bring the crew.

Something tore at his side and he recoiled, slamming his tender back against the wooden post to his left. He groaned in

pain. It felt like Pearson's whip had left a new laceration in his flesh.

A shriek pierced the air next to Bell, accompanied by the sound of tearing flesh and shattering bone. Warm fluid drenched him.

He curled himself into a ball, waiting for the next strike.

It didn't come. Instead, the shelf shook and splintered and he heard the thud of the beast and his bunkmate spilling to the floor.

The slaves' screams and banging frenzy rose to a crazed crescendo. It smothered the sound of the storm outside.

Lantern light flashed over the hull. Sailors tumbled down the ladders. They cursed and turned whips and fists on the Africans.

The sounds of panic subsided.

The lantern's acerbic glare filled his berth. Bell shielded his eyes, steeling himself for the bite of the whip.

Instead, he heard a ragged gasp and Follett's voice.

"Fucking Christ."

Bell moved his hands from his face. The bulky sailor stood outside the berth, mouth gaping, whip dangling in his hand. The sailor next to him lowered his lantern and retched.

The harsh light dimmed, Bell realized what the men had seen.

A slick sheen of blood covered his berth. The beast hadn't taken all of his bunkmate. The man's arms and legs remained, still clasped tight in their manacles.

* * *

Bell gritted his teeth as Hicks smeared ointment into the fresh wound on his side. The creature's claws had raked deep into his flesh, leaving four red gashes that opened like the gills of a fish gasping for air.

As the surgeon stretched linen around his midsection, Bell wondered if the wounds should be stitched. He gasped from the pain as Hicks tied off the dressing.

Pearson hovered over them in the mess. The dripping candle on the table cast shadows into the creases of his face that made him look tired and old beyond his years.

Rain pattered on the cabin roof. Distant lightning flashed blue in the portholes.

"Before that unholy thing found its way below, it took two more of the crew," Pearson said. "Dowd and Thompson happened upon it while it hung over Dunlap's hammock sucking his life out through his open mouth."

Bell's chest grew tight.

"Dowd?" he asked. "It got Dowd?"

"Knocked him down. He hit his head, but he'll survive. The beast eviscerated Thompson, though. Near split him in half with a swipe of its claw."

Pearson looked down, shaking his head as if he disbelieved what he was describing.

"I saw it myself as it fled, Bell. The demon contorted itself easily as a child twists a ragdoll and disappeared into a crack pried between two floor planks. It was like a ghost, something sunk permanently in shadow."

Bell exhaled. A sick feeling seized him.

Nearly a score men and woman had died—some because of the Captain and his cohorts' idiocy, others because he failed to piece together the clues.

"What is the damned thing, Bell?" Pearson asked. "Has the devil descended on this godless vessel?"

Hicks sat glassy eyed at the adjacent bench, swigging straight from the rum bottle. He looked ready to fall over.

"The Africans know what it is," Bell said. "It must have come onto the ship when we were moored. Free them and we can fight this thing together."

"After the toll we've taken on them? Don't be a fool." Lightning flashed outside and Pearson rose, staring out the porthole. He was clearly shaken—the first time Bell had seen him in such a state. "They'll kill us if they get the chance."

"That's all I have," Bell said. "First, you flog me until I'm near death, then you ask for my advice. I'm not going to lick your boots and tell you what you want to hear."

Why exactly had the captain summoned him topside? An apology? Surely not. Because he needed an extra hand to hunt down the *asanbosam*? Injured, Bell, wasn't sure he'd be much use.

The door opened and Bevan strode inside, drenched. He cradled a musket. The *Lombard*'s hull had been heavy with trade firearms on the way to the Gold Coast. It now had few of its own.

Follett and two more of the crew followed him into the cabin, slopping water across the floor.

"The thing clearly isn't topside," Bevan told the captain. He cast a seething glance at Bell. "Why hasn't this mutinous animal been returned to the hold?"

"Because," Pearson said, "the thing has already tasted Bell's blood. I suspect it will want more."

* * *

Bell staggered forward on the end of Follett's rope, hands bound behind his back. The muscles in his legs twitched and threatened to give way as the party swept through the cargo hold.

The crew, save Dowd, who was still in his hammock, were armed with the few weapons they'd managed to assemble from the hold. Some brandished black powder pistols and muskets, the rest blades and icebreaking pikes.

Bell's legs gave way and he fell against a pile of burlap sacks. He held himself up by his shoulder. Between his lacerated back and torn side, he was in too much pain to continue.

"He's practically dead," Bevan said. "Slap him back into the slave hold."

Bell struggled to his feet.

"No. I can continue," he told them, unsure if he actually believed it.

Pearson dug his saber into the deck and shook his head. "This isn't yielding a thing. I see no reason to continue."

"One sweep of the deck," Bell said. "The big African said the beast likes to climb. It lives in the trees."

Pearson looked up. He cocked his head to listen.

"It seems to have stopped raining," he said. "One more sweep. And if that doesn't draw the devil out, you're back in chains below."

* * *

They trudged back onto the deck where the sails beat furiously overhead, animated by the storm's lingering wind. Bell did all he could not to jump as the canvas spoke its wild language of pops and flutters.

The patrol of nine men moved to the port side of the main cabin. Dim light spilled from its portholes. They were close enough that Bell smelled the tallow of the candles burning inside.

Another noise sounded from above. This time, not the whip of a sail but something scraping wood. Bell placed it just behind them. His pulse accelerated.

Follett jerked the rope around Bell's waist then stopped.

"Did you hear that?" Follett scanned the deck.

"The sail," Bell said. "It's just the sail."

He gauged the distance to the open cabin door, wondering if he could jerk the rope from the sailor's hands and make the run.

Another scrape overhead. A sense of dread thick as congealing blood settled over Bell.

He looked upward and a shadow the color of pale gray smoke slithered over the white sail. Bell held his breath and waited for the shape to drop amidst the crew.

Motion cut the air above them. The captain's eyes rose to the rigging and his jaw fell open. Sailors cried out and a musket discharged somewhere to Bell's right.

Follett fumbled to slip the pistol from his belt and the rope around Bell's waist went slack. He dropped to a crouch. The sudden move set off an inferno that blazed through his wounded side and back.

Bell swung his right leg in an arc, sweeping it against Follett's ankle. The bulky man let out a surprised yelp and flopped backward, head striking the deck. His pistol clattered to the timber.

Bell launched himself toward the cabin door. The rope jerked him backward and cut against the gashes in his side. He looked over his shoulder. Follett had dropped his pistol but not the rope, which he now held with both hands.

Bell crawled toward the cabin on his knees, dragging the cursing boatswain with him.

Another musket shot exploded behind him. Bell closed his eyes, expecting to feel a lead ball tear into his back. It didn't.

Shouts of confusion mingled with screams of pain. More shots and the slap of feet on deck boards.

Dizzy with pain, the world spinning around him, Bell struggled forward on his knees. He grimaced against the Follett's bulk and tried to rise.

The pressure against his waist released and he tumbled forward, falling hard against his shoulder.

Bell lay stunned and gasping just outside the cabin door. A new scream, Follett's, had joined the pandemonium. He looked over his shoulder.

The *asanbosam* had pounced on the boatswain. It crouched over him like a panther, baring iron-gray teeth in a twisted snarl. The remainder of its body seemed to have taken on the blackness of the night sky the way a gecko's shifts color.

Follett screamed, throwing ineffectual fists at the creature. It plunged a claw deep into his abdomen.

Behind Follett, at least one more crewman lay sprawled on the deck, his throat broken open and his once-white tunic red as a British soldier's coat.

Pearson stumbled from the melee, dragging his saber in a limp, useless arm. He gripped his shoulder. Blood seeped between clenched fingers.

Bell struggled to his knees, teetering the last few steps into the cabin. He collapsed and kicked the door shut. The hammocks dangled empty, no sign of Dowd.

Another shriek and something slammed into the side of the cabin. The entire wall shook.

Bell straightened his knee to brace the door and scanned the room for the bar. It leaned against the wall two feet to his left. The

door heaved again and a lightning rod of pain shot through his leg. He cried out and wormed his way toward the bar, arms still bound behind him.

The door pushed open and Follett's face showed in the narrow opening, his mouth open in a cavernous scream of fear and pain.

Steely claws raked the air behind him and he collapsed.

Bell slammed the door closed with both feet and wriggled the final distance to the bar. He pushed himself to the wall and felt the plank between his shoulders.

The sounds of chaos continued outside. Another pistol discharged and its payload smacked into the wall nearby.

Bell closed his fingers around the end of the wooden bar and slid up the wall, struggling not to lose his grip as he rose.

Back to the door, he flipped the plank upward, flailing it toward the nearest holding bracket. Get one side in and he could slide it the rest of the way home.

The door buckled against its latch. Wood splintered.

Bell swung the heavy board behind him. His wrists burned like the ropes around them were molten. The plank clunked against the door and slid down, shy of its target.

More screams. Glass cracked behind him.

Cursing, Bell hoisted the bar again. The effort tore at his wounded side. He let out a grunt of pain. This time, though, he felt the bar catch on the bracket.

Bell fell against the wall and shoved the plank with his shoulder. The bar slid home, securing the door.

Bell leaned against the wall, panting for breath.

What remained of a human face smacked the door's cracked glass porthole, leaving a bloody smear. Flesh dangled in rough streamers and only the blue jacket below the screaming, ruined mouth identified it as Pearson.

The wall rocked again and Bell tumbled away.

One of the *asanbosam*'s hooked appendages penetrated the door, surrounded by a blossom of splintered wood.

Blood pooled under the door. It ran red in the grooves of the floor planks, inching toward Bell.

The hook slid back through the hole and Bell clambered into the far end of the cabin, finding a nest between the wall and an ironbound trunk.

A lantern hook jutted from the wall over his head.

Bell climbed onto the trunk and raised his wrists behind him. He leaned backward, trying to catch the hook on his bonds.

The chaos continued outside. The gunshots had ceased, now replaced by rending sounds.

Bell felt a coil of rope catch against the hook. He jerked against it, working to loosen his ties. He suppressed a cry as one abraded his wrists.

Someone pounded on the barred door.

"Bell, open up!" He recognized Bevan's voice, breaking in fear. "Don't let me die out here!"

Bell ignored the call, yanking the ropes against the catch. The upper coil loosened and began to slip.

An eerie quiet settled outside.

"Bell, don't be a fool," the mate pleaded. "We need each other. Let me inside. We'll free the slaves to fight alongside us."

A familiar *thunk* sounded overhead. The sound of hooks sinking into wood.

Another followed.

Then another.

"You can have all the slaves on the ship if you let me in. All of them." Bevan's voice cracked. "That's a goddamned fortune, man!"

Bell's bonds slipped loose and he flung them to the floor. They coiled like a snake at his feet. He climbed from the chest, rubbing the stinging red gashes at his wrists.

Outside, Bevan's begging became incoherent sobs.

The *thunks* sounded across the cabin roof at a slow and measured pace.

They stopped just over Bell's head. He bit his lip and crouched in silence.

He looked up. A biting chill ran along his shoulders as he wondered how long it would take the *asanbosam* to tear a hole in the roof.

Thunk. The creature took another step, moving in Bevan's direction. It continued its slow prowl toward the door.

Bell hurled open the trunk and spilled its contents across the floor. He rifled through them, grabbing a tinderbox and oil flask.

A single black iron key lay among the detritus. Bell dropped it into his pocket.

Bevan banged at the door.

"Don't let the devil take me. Don't—"

Then the mate shrieked incoherently. His cries continued amid a sickening tearing noise like a butcher separating the parts from a chicken with his hands.

Before the screaming stopped, Bell had scrambled into the tiny closet and down the floor hatch into the smuggler's crawlspace below.

Oil flask in one hand, tinderbox in the other, he wriggled through the smothering darkness. He felt the deep slashes of the creature's claw marks beneath him as he crawled.

* * *

Bell slipped into the slave hold, finding its occupants in a noisy state of panic. The men and women sat up in their berths, shouting in myriad languages. Several—Kwame among them—futilely struggled to tear their chains from the wall.

The big tribesman lay sideways on his shelf, teeth bared, using both feet for leverage as he worked to break his bonds. His scarred head turned toward Bell. "What is happening outside?"

"The crew's dead," Bell said. He lit the lantern hanging next to the ladder and slipped the key from his pocket.

He knelt by Kwame and extended the key. The other Africans looked on, eyes wide in anticipation. Kwame extended his arms, giving Bell access to the shackles.

Bell took a deep breath, wondering what the man might do once he was freed. It was a gamble he had to take. His only hope of survival lay with releasing these men and women.

Shaking, he slipped the key into one of Kwame's manacles, then the other. The chains fell to the rough wooden berth with a dull thud.

Bell stumbled backward, expecting the African to lunge.

The man slipped from the wooden shelf, rubbing his wrists. He was a full head taller than Bell, shoulders wider than most doors in the *Lombard*.

Bell stepped back again and bumped into the bulkhead. Kwame glared down at him. The rest of the Africans looked on, bodies tense as if anticipating swift violence.

"Help me unlock the others." Bell held up the key. "The *asanbosam's* coming."

Kwame said nothing. His eyes seemed to burn into Bell.

Bell knew the man was contemplating whether to strike him down. Given his part in the man's subjugation, it was a fate he probably deserved.

"We've got to work together to stop this thing," Bell said. "Then I can't blame you one bit if you cave my head in."

The towering warrior nodded once and grabbed the key from Bell's hand. In that instant of contact, he realized how easily Kwame could have crushed his wrist in one giant fist.

Bell gathered the shit rakes from their wall pegs, handing them to the men and women Kwame freed.

Two of the men, now armed with the wooden hoes, flanked him. Their severe expressions told Bell they were even less happy with him than Kwame. A wide-faced man with a wide gap between his front teeth shouted and shook his finger at Bell. The other, short and broadly built, grabbed for his collar.

Bell backed up, bumping into the water barrel. He put up his hands. "This can wait. We've got an enemy to fight." He pointed upward. "The *asanbosam*."

Kwame released the manacles from a young woman's wrists. The chains clanked to the floor. He stood, calling to the pair of aggressors. Even though he knew a few phrases in Twi, Bell couldn't make out a single word of the rapid exchange. The two men glared at him, pointing and scowling.

Kwame raised his palms, making a loud declaration. He placed his hands on their shoulders and the two men lowered their heads, uttering apparent apologies.

The young woman whom Kwame had just freed handed him one of the hoes. He snapped it in half over his knee. It broke jagged along the shaft forming two rough wooden daggers.

Kwame handed one to the woman, who bore similar scars, these cut into her cheeks. She cut at the air with it, testing its worthiness.

"Now, where is this demon?" Kwame asked. "We kill it together or we die together."

* * *

Bell scaled the rungs to the main deck and dragged himself through the hatch. The rain had ceased and now dawn spilled across the horizon, a spreading pinkish sliver.

The slap of bare feet on wood planks followed him. He sensed the presence of others on the steps behind him and hoped Kwame was between him and the two more hostile men. The group moved silently over the deck, still slick with rainwater.

Bell sensed no movement. Only the hiss of the ocean and the gentle slap of the mainsail broke the stillness.

A single body lay crumpled near the cabin's aft. No, not crumpled, *folded.* Its joints bent in angles a body was not meant to articulate.

By the pistol still clenched in its hand, Bell recognized the corpse as Bevan's. The mate's white pants were now stained deep red. One of his boots lay more than a yard from the body.

Bell looked upward at the billowing white sails and their web of ropes and riggings. The *asanbosam,* sated, could have climbed into a roost somewhere above.

He moved over the deck in a slow crouch, realizing that in his haste to arm the others, he'd grabbed no weapon for himself. That the freed captives had elected not to kill him spoke of their mercy—or perhaps of their fear of Kwame.

The Africans fanned out around him, moving in a slow prowl. The woman whom Kwame armed held her wooden stake at the ready. The muscles in her shoulders and upper arms seemed tense enough to snap.

Bell tapped Kwame's upper arm and pointed to the rigging. "It was up there when it dropped on the crew," he whispered. "Be careful."

Kwame motioned to the men around him and pointed to the rigging overhead. The group continued its forward sweep, eyes darting with every pop of the sails.

The tall warrior advanced on Bevan's corpse and prodded it with his foot. When it didn't move, he tugged at the shoulder with his weapon.

The body flopped over, emptying the contents of its sundered chest cavity with a nauseating splat. Bell turned his head, gagging.

Kwame picked up Bevan's pistol, holding the bloodied handle between two fingers like a soiled garment. He examined it for a second and passed it to Bell.

Bell took a deep breath and knelt beside Bevan. Averting his eyes from the guts spilled across the deck, he felt through the body's blood-drenched jacket for ammunition.

The Africans scanned the rigging overhead. Several had already advanced to the sides of the cabin. Bell found a ball and wadding in Bevan's pocket. A doeskin powder bag dangled from his throat on a thin leather cord.

Bell armed the pistol, making a funnel with his palm to guide the powder into the barrel. He hoped the bag had stopped blood from completely soaking its contents.

A shout sounded from the other side of the cabin. The others raced toward the bow and Bell joined them. As he rounded the corner, his bare feet slid in something warm and slick.

He grabbed one of the porthole shutters, barely keeping himself upright. Blood so thoroughly saturated the deck it seemed like a wave of it had slapped the ship's side.

The Africans pointed and spoke among themselves. Several covered their faces. One man staggered to the rail and vomited into the ocean.

The remains of the crew were stacked in front of the door, assembled into in a grisly totem.

The torn corpses stood back-to-back, lashed together by grayish-pink intestines. A ring of body parts circled them, its centerpiece the captain's severed head. Pearson's mouth hung open, and his severed tongue, glistening and swollen like a purple slug, lay on the deck by his chin.

Kwame stepped forward and rapped his chest with a fist. He shouted to the Africans circling the corpses. Several others also uttered words. Bell presumed some to be prayers, others curses.

The scarred woman entered the cabin and returned with sheets and blankets, which she and the others draped over the bundled corpses.

"What did you say to them?" Bell asked Kwame.

"It's blasphemy," he said. "Not even the evil whites deserve this."

* * *

Bell and the Africans searched the upper decks until they were sure the *asanbosam* no longer lurked topside. The sun reflected red in the waves as if the blood spilled over the side of the *Lombard* had stained the ocean on which it floated.

Bell distributed timber, hammers and nails to the Africans. Together they closed over the slave hold and the trap door into the crawlspace. Such a measure, he knew, wouldn't contain the creature for the duration of their voyage, but it would keep it sealed away long enough to mount a defense.

The scarred woman, whom Kwame called Amma, gathered weapons from the deck. Others dropped the crew's remains overboard and used buckets to clean the timbers of blood and viscera.

When the work was done, they convened in front of the cabin, standing over the small arsenal they had gathered. A musket, two pistols, two sabers and a tangle of mops, hoes and icebreaking pikes lay at their feet.

"Have any of them fired a gun before?" Bell asked.

Kwame addressed the group in Twi, moving his hands as he spoke. He mimed firing a pistol. The men and women shook their heads.

The gap-toothed man who had menaced Bell earlier stepped forward. He muttered and nodded to the musket. Kwame thrust the weapon into his hands.

"Ekow says he has fired one," Kwame said. He knelt and retrieved one of the pistols. It looked like a toy in his massive hand. "His village traded with the white men for guns, just like mine."

Ekow spoke in Twi, glaring at Bell.

Kwame translated. "He says he knows white man's weapons and also his treachery."

The rest of the men and women crouched over the pile choosing weapons. Amma rose, having traded her broken hoe for Pearson's saber. She tested its weight, slashing the air.

"We should form two parties," Bell said. "Start at each end of the cargo hold, sweep through and meet in the middle."

Kwame nodded and spoke to the Africans. Weapons in hand, they listened to the plan. The big warrior swept down his arm, apparently showing the group how to divide.

Ekow wrinkled his forehead. He spoke tersely to Kwame, gesturing with the pistol he'd claimed. His eyes fixed on Bell as he spoke.

"Tell him—" Bell began.

Kwame ignored Bell, turning his back. He exchanged more words with Ekow, and finally appeared to acquiesce to the plan. He motioned several of the Africans to his side.

"He says he will lead one of the groups," Kwame said. "But he said that we must pray before we go below deck. His tribe is good at hunting beasts, but we are not hunting a beast."

* * *

Even in the lantern's glow, the hold had never seemed so dark as when Bell, Kwame and their party descended its bow-side ladder.

The rungs creaked under their weight, the only sound breaking the asphyxiating silence. A smell of damp decay assaulted Bell.

A woman Kwame had addressed as Esi swung the lantern around the hold as they waited for the rest to climb down. Its dim light quivered over the jumble of crates and sacks that choked the long, narrow space. A fat-bellied rat scurried from its perch atop a moldering bag, disappearing into the murk.

A cargo net dangled down the port side of the hold, suggesting that they were walking into the lair of a venomous spider.

The light, Bell realized, gave them away, but there was no way they could risk hunting the creature in complete darkness. A faint flicker from the hold's opposite end signaled the other party had also made its way down.

Bell's eyes jumped between every crook and shadowy spot into which the *asanbosam* might slide. The possibilities for ambush seemed unending. Amid the dense clutter, it would be a near impossible task to spot their adversary. It moved like a ghost and seemed to be able to bend and twist itself into impossibly narrow spots.

Their only hope, Bell thought, was that their presence would draw it out for an attack. Coming at it with sheer numbers from two sides, he suspected, they might—*might*—stand a chance.

The ship pitched and a cargo net swayed. Kwame raised his pistol. Sweat beaded on his brow, the first visible sign of nervousness that Bell had seen from the man.

Bell inched forward and the rest followed, fingers wrapped tightly around their weapons. They moved among the crates and burlap bags, covering five feet, then ten. The creature could be anywhere among the clutter.

Bell's wounds ached as he moved and the moistness of the bandage around his ribs told him the rake from the *asanbosam*'s claws had reopened. He needed rest to heal.

A low scrape sounded to their left and Bell jumped, swinging the cocked pistol. Nothing moved at them from the

cargo piled to their side. He swallowed hard and lifted his finger from the trigger, realizing he'd almost fired it in his panic.

Another faint scrape emanated from the area and Kwame pointed to a square wooden crate roughly four feet in height. The others moved to circle it. Esi raised the lantern.

The toe of Bell's boot struck something as he approached. A clatter of metal on wood spoiled their silence. He looked down and realized he'd sent a bent nail skittering against the side of the crate.

Kwame pointed at the lid. He made no noise but his widened eyes were beacons of dread. Something had pried away all four of the lid's securing nails. Two, bent and pried almost to their points, remained in the wood.

Bell and Kwame positioned themselves next to the crate. The Africans raised their weapons and Bell took aim. The pistol felt cold and clammy in his palm. Sweat stung his eyes.

Kwame slid his fingers under the loosened lid. He licked his lips and looked around the group. The dense silence seemed endless.

Bell held his breath. He nodded a go-ahead and Kwame flung away the lid.

One of the Africans drove his makeshift spear into the box. Another swung an icebreaker.

A scream sounded inside. "Stop!"

Dowd.

Bell lowered his gun. The sailor crouched inside, hands raised. Strands of his long hair hung through the bonnet of linen wrapping his head.

"Get up," Bell said. "You're with friends."

Dowd examined the black faces surrounding his hiding place. He swallowed hard, looking unsure whether that was truly the case.

"Mutiny?" he asked.

"Of sorts," Bell said. "The creature, the *asanbosam*, slaughtered the rest of the crew. You and I are the only ones left."

Kwame craned his neck to examine Dowd. He wrinkled his nose. "Can we trust this one?"

A musket thundered from the other end of the hold, rendering the question moot. Shouts, screams and the sound of combat reverberated among the crates and clutter.

Bell raced toward the melee, grimacing against the growing pain in his side. He made it a few yards before leaning against a barrel to collect himself. Blood seeped through his dressing and spotted his shirt.

Kwame and the others passed him, the slap of their bare feet echoing through the hold. Dowd appeared beside him, a length of pine clutched in his hand like a club.

"Are you alright?" Worry clouded Dowd's face.

Bell didn't answer. He took a long, deep breath and resumed his run toward the combat.

Tendrils of smoke snaked along the narrow canyon of cargo. A spreading orange fire blazed in their path. Esi lay sprawled on the deck, her capsized lantern guttering fuel into the flames.

Beyond the curtain of acrid smoke, black bodies writhed in frenzy, swinging fists and weapons against their shadowy adversary. A musket boomed and someone emitted a jagged shriek.

Dowd stripped his shirt and flailed at the spreading fire. Bell ripped a tarpaulin from a nearby crate and followed suit.

Esi did not move as the flames licked her prone form.

More bodies tumbled into the aisle ahead, Ekow among them. The man clutched his throat, dropping his discharged weapon. Blood bubbled from his mouth.

Bell hurled away the tarpaulin and leaped over the fire, leaving Dowd to finish it off.

The creature moved among the Africans like a deadly dancer, twisting and contorting to avoid jabs from sabers and makeshift spears. Its claws cut the air in gray arcs and two more combatants fell.

In the fire's light, Bell realized the beast was built more like a human than he'd originally thought. It stood little taller than its assailants when erect on its hooked feet, although it seemed more adept springing onto them, pouncing like a deadly cat.

Bell raised his pistol and aimed but Kwame moved into his line of sight, swinging his own weapon like a club. Bell cursed. He held his shot and moved forward, aiming again.

With both hands, the scarred woman Amma drove her saber into the *asanbosam*'s arched back. The creature howled and darted toward the wall, its hooked lower appendages chopping at the deck timbers. The sword's broken blade jutted from its shoulder.

Bell fired. The shot slapped into the creature's shoulder. It twisted and hissed, baring iron-gray teeth, but didn't slow its retreat.

The thing hurled itself onto the hull, scurrying the curvature like a fast-moving spider. A hurled club bounced against the wall, missing by more than a yard.

The *asanbosam* reached the ceiling. It plunged a claw into the timber and ripped through it as easily as if it was shredding cloth.

Bell covered his head and dodged the rain of shredded wood. The broken blade of Amma's saber clattered at his feet.

When he looked up again, the *asanbosam* had flatted itself like dough stretched in a baker's hands. It slithered into the opening.

And was gone.

The groans of the dying echoed in the still hold. At least half of the men and women Bell had freed lay butchered at his feet.

* * *

Two of the creature's victims sprawled on the mess tables, unconscious but still clinging to life. Dowd and Amma worked to bandage their deep wounds. Kwame looked out a porthole, his huge hand clutching a pistol so tightly Bell wondered if its wooden handle might snap.

Excluding Kwame, Amma and the two wounded, only four of the Africans survived the attack below. The three men and one woman clustered on the benches, passing a rum bottle.

Bell read the desperation on their faces.

"The *asanbosam* has drunk the blood of many men." Kwame frowned and examined a pistol lying beside one of the wounded. "Even with guns, it's too strong to kill."

Bell rubbed the back of his neck. Tension knotted his shoulders and his side stung with a new ferocity. He'd found a fresh shirt to cover the bandage, refusing to look down and acknowledge how much worse it bled.

"I hit it with a shot," Bell said. "But I'm not even sure I saw a wound in its body. It's as if the thing absorbed the ball."

Dowd knotted a wounded man's dressing and slid a bottle from the table. He uncorked it with his teeth.

"If we don't figure out some way to finish this thing off, we may not even make it another day." Dowd upended the bottle and guzzled. Rum dribbled down his chin.

"If it kills us all, it's going to be floating in this goddamned bucket, starving," Bell said. "It will run out of blood. But is it smart enough to know that?"

Kwame frowned. "The *griot* said if the *asanbosam* catches a man, it only drinks a little blood at a time. It can feed off one man for many rains."

Dowd flopped down on one of the benches. He wrenched the bandage from his head and touched the scabbed wound at his scalp. His hair stood around his head like a rooster's comb.

"Wonderful," he said, exhaling. "Do we wait around to die or become its feeding herd?"

"We know it likes to feed at night," Bell said. "Maybe our best chance is to find it sleeping below deck during the daytime."

"Maybe it doesn't sleep," Dowd said and took another pull from his bottle. "Have you considered that?"

"It should have been sleeping when we found it in the hold," Kwame said. "Did you not see what it did to us?"

The Africans clustered on the bench watched the conversation. Their eyes seemed to ask Bell the same question. He doubted they understand a word, but they no doubt sensed the dismal tone.

One of them, a wiry man with narrow shoulders, jabbed a long finger toward the floor below and spoke. His words came in an angry tumble.

"Akwasi says he will not follow you down the ladder again," Kwame translated. "Only death awaits us in the hold."

Bell sighed. He had helped kidnap these poor souls, dragged them away from their lands and families. The responsibility wasn't his alone, but he'd taken part. Just as bad, he had failed to protect them when the creature stalked the hold. And, once he'd freed them, he'd led half to their death.

A draining sense of hopelessness settled over Bell. If he simply curled up in his hammock and closed his eyes, maybe the creature would take him in the night. It might bring a quick death, but it wouldn't erase his guilt.

Amma finished wrapping the other woman's wounds. The boards creaked as she walked to Kwame's side. She watched the fore of the ship through the porthole and placed a reassuring hand on the tall man's side.

"We have cannon," Bell said, pointing in the same direction. "A couple of six-pounders in the bow to protect against pirates."

"Cannon are wonderful for firing on other ships," Dowd slurred. He rested the rum bottle on the table. "Fire on the creature, though, and we risk sinking ourselves."

"The powder," Bell said.

"Powder?" Kwame turned away from the porthole, raising an eyebrow. The scars on his head shifted.

"We have a fifty-pound keg of powder for the cannon," Bell said.

"Same problem," Dowd said. "Set off a bomb and we're sunk. Light a smaller quantity and we burn. I'll pass on both."

Bell cursed under his breath. He wondered what the creature was doing while the *Lombard*'s survivors argued.

"Dowd, this brig could sail with a damaged mainmast, couldn't it?" he asked.

Dowd shrugged. "This is my first time out, so I'm hardly the man to ask. But I suppose it could. It would just be a slow slog."

"Look, we know this thing likes to climb. It stalked the crew above." Bell walked to the porthole and looked over Amma's shoulder at the sails flapping against the mast. "If we hoisted the keg to the crow's nest, we could create a trap."

"Even if the powder does not kill the demon, it would fall a long way," Kwame said.

"My first passage out, I saw a sailor lose his footing up there," Bell said. "The body we sewed into the canvas was a shattered tangle. The man was barely recognizable."

"One problem," Dowd said. "How do we get the goddamned beast up there?"

Bell turned away from the porthole, wincing from the pain in his side.

"Someone serves as bait," he said.

* * *

Bell peeled away his bandage in the galley while the others rolled the powder keg on deck. Yellow pus oozed from the wound. He splashed rum onto his side, wincing against the sting, and changed the dressing.

They had searched Hicks' bunk earlier and found his ointment bottle, but Bell refused any. Instead, he'd helped Amma apply it to the Africans' wounds.

They deserved it and he didn't. He had shown the worst kind of arrogance to believe that being from Barbados had somehow made him any better. To take Pearson's praise for anything but condescension.

He felt sick thinking that he'd been willing to sell one of the Africans into bondage so he could buy land and freedom for himself.

Neither of the wounded had come around to consciousness, and the woman's breathing had fallen shallow, almost undetectable. Bell suspected she would die soon.

He went on deck and watched Dowd, Kwame and the rest of the Africans hoist the keg up the mast.

Dowd and Akwasi crouched in the crow's nest, guiding the barrel while Kwame, Amma and the others tugged the rope strung over the topgallant.

Bell grabbed the end of the rope and Amma turned, shaking her head.

"No, George," Kwame said. "You rest and we work."

Bell hesitated. "I owe you an apology," he said. "I am sorry for what I did to you, to all of you. I served on this ship because I needed money. I didn't—"

"You and I are the same," Kwame said. "We trusted the whites. You for money, me for guns and cloth—things for the village. Now we must pay. He who digs a pit for others will always fall in." He gestured toward the rail. "Go now. Rest."

Bell backed away and propped himself against the bulkhead. The sea below swayed gently. He meditated on the hiss, closing his eyes.

He drifted in and out of sleep until the ship rocked, jolting him awake. He looked up at the darkening sky.

Overhead, Dowd and Akwasi secured the powder keg in the crow's nest. The two men looked tiny against storm clouds churning in the distance. The sea chopped the ship's sides and a building wind slapped the sails.

More rain drifted their way. If the clouds burst above them, Bell knew, there was no way they could light the powder. A curse followed the *Lombard*.

Dowd and Akwasi knotted a long rope to the nest and let it uncoil the forty yards to the deck.

The pair clambered down the shroud and approached Bell.

"Whoever gets the creature up the mast had better climb fast," Dowd said. "That fuse is short and the rope down is a fucking long one."

Kwame, Akwasi and Amma joined them at the rail, gazing up at the handiwork. The three other Africans ambled back to the mess.

"Who makes the climb?" Dowd asked. "Do we draw straws?"

"Seems the fairest way," Bell said. "Or someone could volunteer."

Kwame examined the slate-hued sky and rested a hand on Amma's shoulder. "We must find the demon soon. The rains are near. I can smell them."

Shouts sounded from the direction of the mess, then the tinkling of shattered glass. The shouts turned to screams.

Bell and the rest darted for the cabin. The run ignited a fire in his side.

Kwame arrived first and hurled open the door. Two corpses slumped inside, their bare torsos torn open. The throats of the two wounded splayed like gutted fish.

A crimson slick led from the entryway to the center of the room. The *asanbosam*'s sinewy arm protruded from a rupture in the floorboards there, its color perfectly mimicking the reddish wood. The creature's claws sunk deep into the third African's torso. The dead man's limbs jerked as the creature struggled to tug him into the too-narrow opening.

Kwame grabbed the musket from its resting place next to the door and jabbed the bayonet through the creature's forearm. Blue-gray blood jetted onto the floor. He jerked the trigger and blasted away a hunk of its flesh.

The *asanbosam* howled and withdrew its arm. The scratch of clambering claws and hooks reverberated beneath the floorboards.

Bell fired his pistol into the wood after the creature. Wood splinters erupted from the floor, but the shot didn't seem to slow its escape.

"It got back into the crawlspace," Bell shouted. "It spills out at the aft."

"By the privies?" Dowd asked.

Bell didn't answer. He was already out the mess door, the other pistol in hand.

* * *

Bell slid down the ladder into the narrow hallway running behind the slave hold. His throat constricted from the stench of the *Lombard*'s shithouse.

Kwame and Akwasi dropped behind him. Bell held his breath and pointed to an opening in the ceiling, where several boards dangled, splintered to pieces. Droplets of the creature's bluish blood dotted the floor.

Kwame jabbed his bayonet into the opening above and Bell crouched, extending his pistol. Nothing moved in the blackness beyond the sheared timbers.

Akwasi gestured to the floor. The *asanbosam*'s blood led in the direction of the privies. The room's door swung loose on a single hinge. In its haste to escape, the creature must have knocked it loose.

They advanced toward the dangling door. A cold tension crept along Bell's shoulders and back.

The ship gave an abrupt pitch and he steadied himself against the wall. Just ahead, Akwasi flinched at the sudden movement, slashing his saber at thin air.

The man looked over his shoulder, smiling nervously at Bell and Kwame, as if to apologize for his panicked reaction.

Then a faint scratch sounded from inside the room.

Akwasi raised the saber again and kicked the door off the remaining hinge. It clattered into the tiny room. Bell braced himself, expecting the creature to hurtle into the hallway.

Silence.

He and Kwame inched forward. He craned his neck to peer into the tiny room. Flies buzzed in and out of the three bog holes. Spatters of shit painted the walls.

Akwasi took a tentative step onto the fallen door, apparently testing to see whether it had landed on the creature. He entered the room and jabbed his saber into the first of the bog holes.

Surely, Bell thought, taking a shallow breath, the thing wouldn't hide in the begrimed soup down there. He scanned the room and realized that the room's single porthole had shattered. Only a few long shards of glass jutted from the tarnished brass ring surrounding it.

Bell and Kwame slipped into the room.

Akwasi thrust his saber into the next two bog holes. Splashes echoed from below. He shook his head.

Kwame lowered his musket and started in the other direction. "It went the other way," he said.

"Or out there." Bell gestured to the broken porthole. "Back up the side of the ship."

Akwasi apparently had the same thought. He climbed onto the privy shelf and examined the porthole's bent brass ring.

The man ducked his head toward the porthole and Bell's pulse quickened. Icy air seemed to fill the room. The sky outside churned, now ominous as black smoke.

Bubbling sounded beneath Akwasi and Bell flung himself back from the bogs.

A torrent of filth erupted from the middle privy hole and the *asanbosam* launched itself upward, its long arms enveloping Akwasi. The creature's maw opened like a feeding shark's and its iron-gray teeth tore into flesh.

Something heavy hit the floor at Bell's feet and his companion's slight body danced backward, headless. Blood pulsed in red gouts across the walls and floor.

Bell screamed and discharged his pistol without aiming. The shot thundered in the confined space. Searing smoke obscured his vision.

The *asanbosam*'s bulk exploded through the haze and Kwame drove the bayonet into its chest. The tribesman bared his teeth, twisting the musket to drive the blade deeper.

The creature slashed at Kwame. Its claw shattered the wall planks by his head.

"Run!" Bell screamed, realizing he couldn't hear his own voice over the ringing in his ears. "Just run, man!"

He barreled down the hall.

Another shot roared behind Bell but he didn't turn to see the outcome. He was vaguely aware of the vibrations of at least one more set of feet pounding behind him.

He prayed they belonged to Kwame.

Bell scrambled up the ladder to the main deck, almost losing his grip as his boot, wet with waste, slipped from one of the rungs. He caught himself before he fell and felt a tearing in his injured side.

He ignored the pain, found his footing and clambered up the rest of the way.

Breathless, Bell threw himself onto the deck. Crippling pain wracked his side. Fists of rain smacked the planks around him.

Dowd extended a hand and yanked Bell to his feet. The sailor held the pistol Bell discarded earlier.

Kwame tumbled beside him, face contorted in fear. He no longer held the musket.

"Behind us!" Kwame screamed. He scrambled away from the hatch. Amma stepped between him and the open hatch. She braced a broken hoe at hip level like a short spear, its tip sheared to a menacing point.

Bell ripped open his powder bag and shook it over the barrel of his pistol. Half its contents spilled across the wet deck.

He was too late.

The *asanbosam* sailed from the open hatch, landing in the middle of the deck. It bared bloodied teeth and howled. Excrement pooled beneath its hooked feet.

Dowd backed away, slipping the knife from his belt.

The creature pounced and pinned the sailor with its hooked feet. Dowd screamed, flailing with his knife and fist. The creature ignored the ineffective blows and swung its right claw as a cat might bat a mouse.

Blood splashed the deck and Dowd stopped struggling.

Bell finished reloading his pistol. The intensifying rain mingled with spilled black powder, muddying the grip and his hand. He raised the weapon and squeezed its trigger.

The *asanbosam* arched its back, screeching as the slug penetrated its body. Its head swiveled, gray teeth bared their full length.

The creature leaped from Dowd's torn body.

Bell hurled the spent pistol at it and ran for the mast. The sound of the *asanbosam*'s hooks chopping the deck followed him. He slipped on the wet deck and he tumbled, landing hard on his hip. Red soaked through his shirt from the reopened wound.

Bell scurried on hands and knees, launching himself for the mainmast. He dragged himself up the shroud of rope netting. Warm blood mingled with the rainwater, drenching the side of his pants.

He ascended, ignoring the pain. Something slapped his ankle and he almost plummeted. He dangled by his hands for a second,

kicking his legs to find purchase again. He felt as if a pair of unseen hands was twisting him in half.

The *asanbosam*, skin now gray as the roiling storm clouds, advanced up the netting toward him. It pulled back a claw and Bell closed his eyes, bracing to feel daggers driven into his chest.

Instead, a pained howl sounded below and he looked down. Amma had driven her weapon into the beast's back. She twisted it with both hands, her war cry sounding through the rain's insistent percussion.

The *asanbosam* backhanded her and she fell, sliding across the rain-soaked deck.

Her attack hadn't killed the beast, but it bought Bell time. He continued his frantic scramble up the netting. He hooked an arm over a wooden crossbeam and dragged himself onto the maintop. He rose on his knees and looked over the edge.

The creature pried the wooden spike from its back and hurled it across the deck. It climbed after Bell, hissing through its needle-like teeth.

Bell dragged himself up to the boom and reached for the crosstrees.

His right hand slipped from the wooden climbing peg, drenched and slick with rain. As, he guessed, was the powder keg. It would never light.

Bell looked down.

Blue blood bubbled from the puncture in the *asanbosam*'s back. But, even with a gouting wound, the creature gained on him. It seemed to fly across the netting, a spider skittering along its web.

Damn the keg. Bell wouldn't give it the satisfaction of taking him easily.

He grabbed the wet peg again and heaved himself upward. He climbed, squinting against the rain pelting his face. The crow's nest loomed ahead, a beacon amid the drenching storm.

A spasm wracked the whole left side of Bell's body and he misjudged his footing. His boot slipped from a rain-soaked peg. He dangled by his fingers, felt their grips weaken.

Pennsylvania, Alice, the Rembert plantation, all seemed to melt away in the torrent. All that mattered now was the debt he owed the Africans.

"Not now," he groaned through clenched teeth. "Please, not yet."

The deck disappeared under a squall from the turgid sea and the mast swayed as if the ship were capsizing. Bell screamed as he hung by fingertips.

The *Lombard* righted and he cycled his legs until one boot heel, then the other, found pegs again. He scaled the mast, grunting in pain as he fought his way up each rung.

He closed the remaining yards to the crow's nest and tumbled inside, wheezing. His back rested against the soaked powder keg. The ache in his arms and shoulders rivaled that of his wounded side.

Thunder clapped overhead and another wave shook the ship. Bell dug his fingers into the nest's wooden bucket. The churning black sea rocked the vessel hard to its side.

The mast dipped to a 45-degree angle and the chopping waves loomed huge.

For what seemed like a frozen lifetime, Bell hung, wondering whether his doom would come in the cold depths or from the beast trailing him up the mast.

The ship righted and Bell let out a sigh.

A thrashing sound cut short his second of relief and the nest shook, threatening to break loose. Splinters showered him. He watched in paralyzed fear as iron talons shredded the starboard side of his roost.

The *asanbosam* grinned through the ruined wood. Its eyes glinted like globes of onyx. Its jaw gaped like it planned to swallow Bell whole. Its breath hit him, hot and rank.

The ship lurched again and Bell scrambled for a handhold. He felt the damaged bucket sway backward, as if his weight might dislodge it from the mast.

The creature hissed. It lost its grip and dropped backward. The leering face disappeared from view and Bell realized it now dangled from its right claw.

Bell wedged himself behind the keg, sliding it toward the *asanbosam*. He lifted himself onto the lip of the nest, resting his backside on the undamaged portion.

The ship flopped sideways again and his guts seized. For the instant it took him to dig his fingernails into the edge of the nest, it seemed like he was suspended in midair, more than a hundred feet over the deck.

The mast rocked back in the other direction and the *asanbosam*'s broad head rose over the broken side of the nest. Its empty black eyes loomed like openings to the cold void of Hell.

Bell thrust both feet against the powder keg and kicked it forward, screaming. It caromed off the creature's head.

Its claws tore through the floor of the nest, shredding the wood as it plunged backward into space.

Its howl slashed through the calamitous noise of the storm. Its long arms and hooked legs jerked wildly as it plummeted.

Bell looked over the edge of the crow's nest. The creature lay in a mangled knot below. Kwame and Amma, tiny from this height, circled its unmoving form.

It too seemed so small from the top of the mast. Had he not seen the carnage it left in its wake, Bell wouldn't believe it could kill so many.

Kwame, then Amma, prodded the dead thing with their weapons and dragged the corpse toward the side of the ship. A trail of dark blue blood followed, as if the thing's dark soul drained from its every pore. The color drained from its ruined body until it was the dead gray of a bloated tick.

The Africans heaved the corpse off the *Lombard* and it sunk into the froth below.

Bell rolled onto his back. He let the cooling rain wash away the memories of where he had been and who he thought he was.

* * *

Bell leaned against the *Lombard*'s wheel, hoping Kwame and Amma didn't notice he wasn't as much steering the ship as holding himself up on weakening legs.

He had barely been able to stand as the trio slid the canvas-sheathed remains of their companions into the deep. It was, he'd told the Africans, the most dignified farewell American sailors knew how to give.

They had mopped the deck of blood, cleaned as much of the filth from the lower hold as they could manage, but the ship still stank of death, fear and sullied humanity.

The wind blew from the West, filling the sails, and if Bell had read the stars and Pearson's maps correctly, it would carry them to a spot on the Gold Coast occupied by neither British nor Dutch.

They could leave the cursed vessel and its stench in two days' time.

The ache burned in Bell's side as he steadied the wheel. The smell of his wound told him it had grown worse.

Kwame's rugged hand slipped onto his shoulder. The tall man stood behind Bell. His other arm circled Amma's waist.

"You are pale, George," he said. "You must rest."

"Let me show Amma how to steer the ship," he said. "That way, one of you can watch during the day and the other at night."

"What about you, George?"

He ignored the question and motioned for Amma. She slipped from Kwame's arm and slid next to Bell at the wheel. He guided her hands into position and she gave it a tentative tug to steady the rudder. Bell nodded to her.

Bell lifted his hands from the wheel as Amma confidently gripped its spokes. She looked over her shoulder, worry in her face.

There was nothing to worry about.

Bell extended his arms. The breeze tickled his fingertips, cooled his face. White clouds rose high in the sky like spun sugar.

They were heading home. He was heading home.

* * *

Kwame helped Amma down the thick rope dangling from the leaning ship. Its wooden side, split on the rocks, looked like the opened belly of a hunted animal.

The chopping surf made the stones slick. The water smelled of salt. The shadows of the tall masts behind them pointed to the shore. The wind beat the sails like drums.

In the distance, sand and rock gave way to tall grasses and broad green watapuo trees.

Amma took Kwame's hand and they steadied each other on the rocks. As one, they stopped.

"We should go back for the body," she said.

"He deserves to be buried with ceremony, not left to rot in the white men's stinking prison," he agreed.

She watched him climb the rope and disappear over the deck. Then she moved closer to the shore.

The smells of the grass and salty surf replaced the reek of the ship. She could imagine the scents of cooking fires.

They would seek the smoke from those fires, and she knew there would eventually be a river. And along that river, eventually a village, and there, a *griot*.

She and Kwame would ask the *griot* to sing a praise song for the black sailor George Bell.

THE END

Sanford Allen, at various times, has worked as a newspaper reporter, a college journalism instructor and a touring musician. He currently divides his creative energy between writing tales of horror, science fiction and dark fantasy and his band Hogbitch, which wallows in the murky swamp between doom metal and space rock. He lives in San Antonio, Texas, with his wife Tracey. This is his first novel. www.sanfordallen.com